Before you read *The Sandfather*, here's what readers
have said about Linda Newbery's Nestlé Award-
winning novel *Catcall* . . .

I wanted to read for hours on end because the book
kept me on the edge of my seat.

A fantastic ending! I love the way the author so richly
describes the characters.

It's an action-packed book and it's got scenes when
you just want to read on.

It grips you to the pages and is definitely quite scary in
some parts.

It is as if you are stepping into the character's body and
seeing everything happen . . . I have no idea where she gets
her ideas from, but she is definitely a genius.

It is a haunting book that hooked me in from the first line.

For more information about Linda's writing – or to
tell her what *you* thought about
The Sandfather – visit www.lindanewbery.co.uk

Brinton £5 24

The Sandfather

LINDA NEWBERY

Illustrated by
Ian P. Benfold Haywood

Orion
Children's Books

First published in Great Britain in 2009
by Orion Children's Books
a division of the Orion Publishing Group Ltd
Orion House
5 Upper St Martin's Lane
London WC2H 9EA
An Hachette Livre UK Company

3 5 7 9 10 8 6 4 2

A catalogue record for this book is
available from the British Library.

ISBN 978 1 84255 548 4

Typeset at The Spartan Press Ltd,
Lymington, Hants

Printed and bound in Great Britain by
Clays Ltd, St Ives plc

The Orion Publishing Group's policy is to use papers that
are natural, renewable and recyclable products and
made from wood grown in sustainable forests. The logging
and manufacturing processes are expected to conform to
the environmental regulations of the country of origin.

www.orionbooks.co.uk

To the memory of Maggie Noach,
literary agent and friend

CONTENTS

Hal was trying to run – stumbling, floundering, his feet sinking into loose sand. Ahead, the Sandfather walked away, surer-footed, his outline blurred against the dazzle of sea. He was made of the same stuff as the beach: fine, glittering grains, moulded into man-shape. He belonged here.

Hal tried to shout 'Wait!' but the word lodged in his throat.

The Sandfather didn't pause, or look back. He splashed into the shallows, then waded in deeper. The waves tugged at him, fretted and sighed, washed at him and over him. Dissolved him.

Hal stood helpless on the shore. Now there was nothing to show where the Sandfather had been: only the sea's vastness, and the long curve of the bay.

1

SHOVE

Hal blamed Luke. Luke blamed Hal.

Afterwards, trying to account for himself in the Year Head's office, Hal couldn't explain how annoyance had exploded into rage, how it had taken him over. How Luke had goaded him to the point of lashing out in fury. Wanting to hit. Wanting to hurt.

Luke didn't know when to stop; that was the trouble. Those things he kept saying about Mum, about Grandad – like a wasp that had got inside Hal's shirt and was stinging him, burning and branding him, while he swatted in vain.

The corridor at lesson change-over time – with the flow of bodies in both directions, people dawdling, people pushing past – was hardly the best place for a fight. But all Hal could see was the smug expression on Luke's face. It filled his mind, maddened him.

It began with a shove, and, through clenched teeth, 'Shut it, will you? Just shut it!' But the push was harder than he intended. Luke, unbalanced by his rucksack, fell heavily against a window-ledge. Righting himself, he directed a murderous glare at Hal, then shrugged off the rucksack and leapt at him.

'*Fight! Fight! Fight,*' chanted eager voices. And now Hal and Luke faced each other like gladiators in an arena, surrounded by faces keen with excitement or alarm. Luke's expression was a taunt.

Osman tried grabbing Hal's arm. 'Pack it in, you two!'

'Go for it, Marbles!' a voice shouted; another jeered, 'Watch out, he'll go mental.'

Hal didn't look to see who'd called out. He launched himself, whamming his fist into the softness below Luke's ribs. Luke doubled up, but recovered with a head-butt that slammed into Hal's chest, winding him. Then it all got messy – scrabbling and grappling for holds, trying to kick, to wrestle free.

'Boys, boys!' said a female voice.

Dimly Hal registered that another body was intruding, a hand on his shoulder, pulling; a waft of perfume reached his nose. He lurched and toppled; hearing a gasp, he shifted his focus from Luke's next move, and saw a frail figure stagger back to collide hard with the wall, then crumple.

Books, bag and stick were strewn across the carpet. She'd fallen awkwardly, like a dropped puppet. Her skirt had flared out above her knees, revealing legs that looked too thin for the clumpy shoes she wore.

Ms Kenwood. Who had to walk with a stick because of arthritis or something.

It seemed all wrong – wrong and suddenly more serious, an adult disaster forcing its way into a private quarrel. Ms Kenwood seemed too shocked to get up, even to try; only her eyes moved in her pale face.

There was a moment of frozen silence. The other kids had backed away, leaving Hal and Luke exposed. Fights weren't unusual, but knocking over a teacher – a *disabled* teacher – was unheard of. What if she was injured? Something broken? She looked frail enough for an arm or a leg to snap.

'Christ!' Luke muttered. 'You've done it now, Marbles.'

Someone giggled nervously. A corridor-jam was building up in both directions, as people tried to move along, or were drawn by curiosity. Only now did time seem to jolt itself forward again.

An older girl moved to help Ms Kenwood – 'Miss! Are you all right?' – and Osman began to pick up the scattered books and belongings.

'I – I think so.' Ms Kenwood gave a weak smile. 'If you could just – oh—'

Hal couldn't move, couldn't think. He felt big and clumsy, faintly dizzy: mind whirring, eyes not quite seeing. He might have been watching something in a play or on TV, nothing to do with him. How had this happened?

'What's going on here? Let me through.' This voice belonged, unmistakably, to Mrs Stanley, Head of Year Nine. The barricade of watchers parted to let her through, and at once she was in charge. She stared, taking in Ms Kenwood on the floor, now being helped gingerly to her feet by the year-ten girl, then her pale eyes swerved to Hal and to Luke, who reached up a hand to straighten his tie.

'Get along to your lessons, all of you,' Mrs Stanley said. 'No, not you, Hal. Nor you, Luke. To my office.'

Was she telepathic, or what? How did she know Ms Kenwood hadn't been taken ill, or fainted? But she *did* know. She was one of those teachers no one ever thought

3

of disobeying. At once, the corridor traffic began to move smoothly in both directions, people keeping to the left, as they were supposed to. Mrs Stanley turned to Ms Kenwood, who was standing unsteadily, supported by the girl. Osman had given her back her stick, and now, at Mrs Stanley's instruction, was fetching a chair from the nearest classroom.

'What are you two hanging round for?' Mrs Stanley snapped at Hal and Luke. 'I said go to my office. Wait there till I come.'

Ms Kenwood looked weak and dithery; she stood clutching one elbow. Was her arm broken, elbow dislocated? All because . . . Hal tried to replay the incident in his mind; wished he could go back and wipe the whole thing, start again.

Luke turned to go. Hal dithered, feeling that he ought to speak.

'Uh . . . sorry,' he mumbled.

Ms Kenwood's eyes were big and swimmy. She looked about to speak, but Mrs Stanley got in first. 'I should hope you *are* sorry! At the very least. I'll deal with you in a moment.'

He followed Luke. Neither spoke until they reached reception; then Luke said, in an undertone, 'Look, it was an accident, right? You didn't mean to do it.'

'What do you mean, *I* didn't?' Hal flared. 'What about you?'

'Yeah, right – blame me, why don't you?' Luke flung back. 'You're the one who's losing it—'

His face was doing that mocking thing again, that sneer that acted on Hal like an electric goad. Anger coursed through him all over again. He grabbed the strap of Luke's rucksack and yanked it hard; letting out a yelp, Luke was flung off-balance. Hal twisted him in a head-lock. In a voice that didn't sound like his own, he snarled into Luke's ear, 'Lay off – got it? Just leave me alone.'

'Loser!' Luke's voice came back, muffled by Hal's arm.

Hal raised his knee, getting a satisfying *ooomp* from Luke. But there was a wheezing gasp as the automatic doors parted, and now here was the suited figure of the Head. The receptionist had scuttled out from behind her glass hatch, and a visitor, a woman with a sharp, peevish face, was staring from a low chair by the noticeboard. Hal had lost all sense of his surroundings, but now they sprang out at him in vivid colour – the art displays, the Head's red tie, the visitor's bright green raincoat.

What was he *doing*?

'Stop that at once!' barked the Head, as if Hal wasn't already as still as a waxwork.

'I saw what happened, Mr Blake.' The receptionist stepped forward, darting nervous looks at each face in turn. 'This boy here just flew at this other one, and started wrestling him.'

Mr Blake frowned. 'Marborough, isn't it? Hal Marborough. And—?'

'Luke Spicer,' Luke supplied.

'I do apologise for this,' Mr Blake said smoothly, turning to the visitor. 'Excuse me just one moment.' Then, to the boys, 'Wait here. And smarten yourselves up, both of you.' He indicated the precise spot where they were to stand.

Hal looked down at the carpet. His brain was throbbing; hot tears would burst out of him if he tried to speak.

You've done it now, Marbles, Luke had said. And probably he had.

2
HALF

As always, Hal went into JJ's to tell Mum he was home. He opened the door to the hot, scented air inside, the busy sound of driers, and Radio 1 cheerful in the background. Mum was there, with a customer, busy with comb and scissors and conversation.

Usually he went straight to Mum, even if she had a client, but this time he stood in the reception area and waited for her to see him. She glanced his way, quickly excused herself and came over. She gave him her usual kiss and arm-rub, and he thought for a moment that she didn't know. But then she said, 'Mrs Stanley phoned.' Just that: no more.

'Uh.' Hal didn't trust himself to speak. Was everyone looking at him? He felt hot and awkward. Too big, too male in this feminine place.

'You go on up. We'll talk about it later. All right?'

Hal nodded, swallowing hard.

'There's carrot cake if you're hungry. See you in a bit.' Mum turned back to her client; Jacky, the salon owner, gave Hal a big grin and a wave.

Mum always wanted to know everything about his day – what lessons he'd had, how he'd done in PE, whether he'd been praised for good work or effort. But *this* day he wanted to forget. There was no way he could keep it from Mum, though: not if Mrs Stanley had been on the phone.

'You know how things stand, Hal,' she'd told him in her office. 'You've been in here often enough. But you just don't seem able to control yourself. I'll have to take it further.'

Outside, he went along the row of shops, through the door between the newsagent's and the fish-and-chip shop, and upstairs to the flat. *Take it further.* What did that mean – chuck him out of school? Mum couldn't know quite how bad it was, not yet, or she wouldn't have been talking about carrot cake. He had the sense of having crossed a line. Mrs Stanley usually finished her telling-off with a joke and a smile: a rather fierce one, but still a smile. There'd been no smile today, no lightening of tone. And he hadn't been allowed back into lessons. He'd spent the whole afternoon in Mrs Stanley's office, working by himself, or at least pretending to work while he fretted about what would happen next.

Course, it wasn't as bad for Luke. Luke was in trouble too, but he hadn't had all those warnings; hadn't been hauled up to the Year Head's office several times before. Besides, Luke could blag his way out of anything.

Hal didn't want to think about Luke. He dumped his rucksack in his room and changed into jeans and hoodie. For once he hung his blazer and trousers in the wardrobe instead of flinging them over the back of a chair; he'd better start getting *some*thing right.

7

Into his mind flashed the picture of Ms Kenwood sprawled and winded, and the fear in her eyes – fear of what being knocked over might do to her. Mrs Stanley had made sure Hal was well aware of that. It wasn't like someone pushed over in a game, who'd just get straight up and carry on playing. Mrs Stanley had wanted to call an ambulance, to get Ms Kenwood to A & E, but Ms Kenwood insisted that there was no need, nothing broken. Still, her husband had been summoned from work to drive her home and look after her.

Whoever's fault all this was, it definitely wasn't *hers*. With a wincing shrug, Hal tried to blank her out of his thoughts.

He turned on his PlayStation, but couldn't summon any interest; switched on the TV, but found nothing to hold his attention; wandered round the flat, and stopped at his reflection in the bathroom mirror.

Still, sometimes, his face surprised him, though he ought to know what it looked like by now. But often he thought he knew only half of it. Half of himself.

There were glimpses of Mum in the face that looked back at him: the slim nose, the well-defined lips. But the rest was different – the dark brown eyes (Mum's were blue), the dark curly hair (Mum's was brown, with copper highlights). And the *skin*. Beautiful skin, Mum said, quite without blemish. Not fair and prone to sunburn, like hers. Not black either, but somewhere in between. Caramel, she said. Or good strong coffee. Or crème brûlée. Or toast done to the perfect degree of brownness. Good enough to eat, she was always telling him.

But half of him was missing. The black half. His father's half.

At school Hal wanted to think of himself as black, but everyone knew he had a white mother. How could he be one of the black boys, when there was no one black in his family? Dual heritage, he was called now. But the dual heritage people in his form included Kazumi who was half-Japanese and Jazza who was half-Indian. Neither was like him, and they both had two parents, so knew what their different halves were. All Hal knew was that his missing half was Afro-Caribbean. He was proud of that, but he wanted more. Wanted something to get hold of and keep.

Who is he? Hal asked his reflection. Who's my Dad? *Where* is he? Does he know about me?

Mum would never tell him, no matter how he pleaded.

'Don't *you* know who he is? Is that it?' he would try.

That always made her hesitate, so that Hal thought she'd have to give in. She didn't want him to think there could be several possible fathers – what would *that* say about her? But if she denied it and said yes, of course she knew, then why wouldn't she tell him?

She did know. Hal knew she did. So why couldn't she just say?

'Why do we live here?' he'd asked her once. 'Is it cos my dad's from here?'

Mum had looked startled, then her face took on the shut, obstinate look he recognised too well. 'No, no, he isn't. Why are *we* here?' For a second she looked unsure. 'Well – it just turned out that way. I got a job and a flat, and it suited us, and we've stayed. I suppose one day we could live somewhere else. Where would *you* like to live?'

She made it sound as if he could choose anywhere he fancied: a New York penthouse, a castle, a ranch.

'By the sea,' he said. 'I'd like to live by the sea. Like you used to.'

Mum gave a small sigh, as if she'd like that too.

Still, at least he knew not to look at every black man he saw around town or at Powerleague or at the leisure centre, wondering if one of them might be his dad. It had been a game he'd always played, sometimes with Luke, until Luke had turned traitor. That one there. No, that one. No, too young, too old. No, he's someone else's dad. Hal didn't want to share his dad with anyone.

Now he went back to his bedroom and reached an arm under his bed, groping through the muddle of discarded games, DVDs and an odd football sock. His fingers met with soft fabric, and underneath it the grating chink of glass.

Carefully he drew out the cloth bag that contained his marbles. This was all he had, the only thing he could take out and look at, actual evidence that his father had ever existed – apart from his own body, his own self, which felt real enough. He took out a marble and held it in his palm, looking into the strange swirl of purple-red, like a slick of wet paint trapped glistening and alive in the glass. Some of the marbles were amber, or deepest blue, or misty-white; some were spangled, shot with gold specks that glinted in the light.

They seemed to hold a promise, a secret. When he was little, he used to put one in his mouth, like a gobstopper, and roll it over and over, tasting its cool curves, its heaviness. Sometimes he'd hold two in his mouth, one each side, so that his cheeks bulged out like a hamster's. Mum used to tell him off for that, in case he swallowed one by mistake, so he only did it when she wasn't looking. The marbles had started off as hers, but she'd given them to him years ago, and told him in an unguarded moment that they'd been a gift from his father. It had been a sort of joke, she said, because she'd had the nickname Marbles when she was at school, just as Hal did now.

A bag of marbles. It wasn't a substitute for a real live father.

Still, Mum had kept them, and that must prove she didn't *hate* the man who had become his father. And he'd given her a present, even if it was only marbles.

Does he know about me? Does he even know I exist?

Hal didn't play with the marbles any more, didn't put them in his mouth, but he liked to know they were there, proof of something.

Restless now, he put the bag back in its hiding place and roamed from bedroom to lounge to kitchen, opened cupboards and closed them, rang Osman's number on his mobile then cancelled it, poured some juice and forgot to drink it. He still had to go through today's incident with Mum, and she'd want to know every single thing. She was quick to weigh in on his side if she thought something was unfair; but today he'd crossed that line, blundered over it to where even Mum's support might be withdrawn.

Mum looked tired as she let herself in at the front door. She dumped three bags of shopping in the kitchen, kissed Hal again and put on the kettle.

'I need a cup of tea,' was all she said, opening the cupboard for a mug. 'Oh, you didn't start on the cake. Weren't you hungry?'

Hal shook his head. He wanted to get it over with, but first Mum put away every item of shopping and changed out of the black clothes she wore for work – all making for an agonising build-up. Then, at last, she took her tea into the lounge, and said, as if she'd only just thought of it, 'We need to talk about what happened today, don't we?' Sagging into her favourite chair, she motioned Hal to sit on the sofa.

'Well,' he faltered. 'It was Luke, winding me up like he always does . . .'

At once he heard how pathetic he sounded, like a little kid bleating excuses: *It wasn't my fault, he started it, it's not fair* . . . How useless words were, the only words he could find! They couldn't begin to show Mum how infuriating Luke could be, how he mocked with an upward roll of his eyes, or a whining imitation of something Hal said.

He faltered through his account. Mum listened, nodding, while he gave an edited version of how Luke had wound him up (he couldn't *tell* her, not what Luke had actually said!) and of not even seeing Ms Kenwood till she was mixed up in the fight.

She didn't say anything at all till he'd finished, and even then she left a long, weighty silence. She pressed her lips together hard, as if she might cry if she let her face do what it wanted. Then she said, 'Hal, this is serious. You do know that? It's not just a squabble between you and Luke. That poor teacher knocked over and hurt, when she was only trying to stop you from hurting yourself or anyone else – you can't just shrug it off and say she got in your way!'

Hal looked down at his trainers, scuffing his toes together. Nothing he said could make it unhappen.

'I'm going to get supper now,' Mum said, 'and I want you to sit down and write a letter to Ms Kenwood, apologising. That's the first thing. And you've got to mean it.'

'Couldn't I just—' Hal wasn't very good at writing letters.

'No. Write a proper letter. It's the least you can do. Write a rough version first and then copy it out in your best writing.'

Mum fetched a pad of writing paper and some loose pages torn out of a notebook for the draft. She began to chop onions for Bolognese, while Hal unscrewed his pen top and chewed his bottom lip. Staring at the blank paper, he drew a doodle that started to look like a face.

'Get on with it, Hal,' Mum said, with her back to him, while she tipped the onions into a pan.

Dear Ms Kenwood, Hal wrote. *This is to say I am very sorry for what happened in the corridoor today I didnt even see you and I didnt mean to knock you over. I know you were only trying to stop me and Luke fighting and you could of got hurt much worse but it wasnt your fault.*

He paused, thinking of brittle bones snapping, of ambulance sirens, and hospital beds. At least it hadn't been *that* bad – but, as both Mum and Mrs Stanley had pointed out, it was only his luck that she hadn't been hurt more seriously, needing hospital. Being knocked over must be awful if you were as frail as she was, with her lurching walk, and her built-up shoe. Hal had thought arthritis was an illness old people got, but Ms Kenwood was younger than Mum. There was something bird-like about her, as if her bones might easily snap. What if something *had* snapped? And it was his fault?

How could he say sorry for that? But what else could he say?

I am really sorry, he wrote again, *and I wish it hadnt of happened*.

Again, he couldn't make the words mean what he wanted. He wished, he really did wish, he'd seen her in time to stop hammering away at Luke. And that wasn't only because he was in trouble now. He liked Ms Kenwood, liked her sudden smiles and the way she made him feel good about himself. She'd done the Black History Month special assembly, and she'd put posters all over her classroom. 'We've been doing a lot about slavery lately,' she'd said, 'but black history isn't *all* about slavery.' She'd told them about Arnaldo Tamayo-Méndez, the first person of African descent to fly into space, and about Andrew Watson, the first black footballer to play for Scotland, more than a hundred years ago. And she'd shown them a website where they could look up ninety-eight more black firsts. She was OK, Ms Kenwood.

But now, when he pictured her face – pale with shock, or pain, or both, as if she couldn't believe this had happened – he could only feel bad, ashamed. And angry at Luke all over again.

Best wishes, Hal Marborough, he finished.

Mum read the letter, corrected the punctuation and spelling and changed *could of* to *could have,* then said he could copy it out neatly.

Was that it, then? His punishment? Had he got off so lightly?

'Now,' said Mum, when he'd written Ms Kenwood's name on the envelope she gave him. 'About tomorrow. You won't be going to school at the usual time.'

He looked at her.

'It's serious, Hal, like I said. We've got a meeting with Mr Blake and Mrs Stanley at ten o'clock. You're not allowed back into lessons till they've decided what to do.'

'What, they're chucking me out?'

'I don't know, Hal. I don't know,' said Mum. She was blinking back tears as she went to the fridge for tomato purée to add to the mince and onions in the pan.

The idea played itself in his head: unreal, almost thrilling. They wouldn't, would they – they couldn't! He wasn't evil, wasn't malicious, wasn't even deliberately disruptive. He just got into situations where the only thing to do was lash out. No matter how many detentions, how many tellings-off, how many warnings, he just couldn't stop himself. His body seemed to act on instinct. Then the rush of satisfaction in his own power – seeing someone sprawling, or doubled up – before his brain kicked in with the knowledge that he wouldn't get away with it, that every incident was making things worse. Luke, or Jason Green, or whoever it was, they always won in the end, by pushing him that bit too far but holding back themselves. He ought to know by now.

'I'll do my best – we both will,' said Mum, stirring the sauce. 'And a lot depends on how you behave at the meeting. Hal, you've got to show you know you were in the wrong. But maybe they've already decided.'

Then what? Hal wanted to ask, but didn't. What if he *was* chucked out, for good? Mum would find him another school, he knew that; he wasn't stupid enough to think he'd be excluded for ever and ever. But if he did start somewhere new, he'd go with a Reputation. With his card marked. The teachers would be watching him, waiting for him to explode. Waiting for their chance to get rid of him. If he started on that path – or was he already on it? – it'd be hard to step off.

How had he got this far into trouble? He hadn't chosen it – trouble seemed to be following him, like a vicious dog, driving him into corners he couldn't get out of.

It wasn't Mum's way to dwell on bad things. They'd have their conversation, she'd say what she needed to say, but she wouldn't go on and on about it, or freeze him out all evening. While they ate their meal, she told him about the customers she'd had today: one who was going to Australia, and another whose son had just started at a specialist sports college, which Mum thought Hal might consider in a year or two, after year eleven. But this brought them back to the fate hanging over him: maybe leaving school, *this* school anyway, without getting as far as GCSEs.

Usually he joined in with bits and pieces from his day, but now he didn't feel like talking. It was an effort even to eat his dinner – the tangy, tomatoey sauce that usually he liked so much was hard to swallow, and the strands of spaghetti seemed intent on twirling themselves off his fork before he could get them to his mouth. He could easily have given up and gone to bed hungry, the way he felt.

When they'd finished, Mum insisted that he did his homework straight away, so that he'd have his books to show at the meeting with all work up to date.

At bedtime he checked his mobile and found a message from Osman: WOTS GOING ON?

TELL U 2MORO, Hal sent back. He'd be staying at Osman's next week while Mum was away. He tended not to get into trouble while he was with Osman; Luke was the problem.

Tomorrow, though? This time tomorrow, after Mr Blake and Mrs Stanley had finished with him, everything might be different.

3
EXCLUDED

'It was just fortunate,' said Mr Blake, seated behind an enormous desk, 'that Ms Kenwood wasn't actually injured. Still, she'd have been quite entitled to take time off work to recover.'

'Hal really is sorry,' Mum put in. 'Aren't you, Hal?'

Hal nodded. They'd already been through this; when would they get to the point?

'Yes, I know,' said Mr Blake. 'And Ms Kenwood insists, Hal, that your aggression wasn't actually directed at her, and that's partly why things aren't quite as serious for you as they might have been.' He looked down at his papers. 'So, Ms Marborough, Hal, this is what we've decided.'

Hal didn't want to hear. He looked down at his shoes.

'We're giving Hal a fixed-term exclusion,' Mr Blake went on, 'starting now and for the whole of next week. That means it'll run into the half-term break. Of course we'll expect Hal to keep up with homework set by his teachers, and to present his work for marking when he comes back at the beginning of November. And he must agree to attend Anger Management sessions for a while, with a specialist.'

Anger Management? What on earth was that? But being excluded – it sounded like an extra week of holiday, whatever they said about work. Beginning of November! It was so far away that he needn't even think about it.

'But what about the football?' he managed to say.

'What was that, Hal?' Mr Blake sat forward, a hand cupped round his ear – a reproach to Hal for mumbling.

'The football,' Hal repeated, loudly and emphatically, just short of being rude. 'I'm playing for year nine on Tuesday.'

'Well, I'm sorry.' Mr Blake shook his head in fake regret. 'Not now, you're not. Someone else can take your place. It's a shame to let Mr Barnes down, and your team mates, but that's part of being excluded, I'm afraid.'

He didn't have to sound so *pleased* about it, Hal thought – this unplanned extra punishment. Missing the football meant far more to Hal than missing school. And he knew exactly who'd be taking his place – Jason Green, the slimy little git. Hal could already see him punching the air when Mr Barnes told him he'd be in.

'So,' said Mum, 'the exclusion is for just one week?'

'Yes. But of course his behaviour will be under review, and, Hal, if you get involved in any more incidents like this, you *could* be excluded permanently. You must understand that.'

'What about Luke?' Mum asked. 'Is he out of school for a week, too?'

'No.' It was Mrs Stanley who answered. 'I've spoken to Luke's parents, and if he gets into more fights, he could be excluded like Hal. But, you see, Hal's already had several warnings. We do follow a set procedure, to make things fair.'

'Yes, I see,' Mum said stiffly. 'I think, Hal, you'd better stay away from Luke when you come back. Don't sit next to him in lessons. Osman's far more sensible.'

'Yes, Osman's a good boy,' Mrs Stanley said. 'I don't know what's gone wrong with you and Luke, Hal, but it's not doing either of you any favours.'

Hal shuffled on his seat, but said nothing. He hated Luke sometimes, all the more because Luke was supposed to be his friend. Or had been. It had always been the three of them together – Hal, Luke and Osman – till things had started to go wrong. Osman was never drawn into taking sides, but was getting fed up with it.

'I'm sure this'll all blow over,' Mrs Stanley said cheerily, 'and you'll be best of friends again.'

Yeah, right.

'We'll arrange another meeting, then,' said Mr Blake, 'for the Monday morning after half-term. If you could both come in at eight-thirty, Ms Marborough, Hal can go straight into lessons for that day after we've met. As long as all's well, of course.'

Mum agreed, and made a note of the date and time, and that was it. They made their way back to reception, where a package of books and worksheets had been left for Hal to take home.

As they walked out to the car park, Hal felt his spirits lifting. Mum might think this was desperately awful, but how bad *was* it, really? A week off school was a week off school, even if it did mean missing Tuesday's match. Almost a double half-term holiday! He looked back towards the windows of the maths block, where his class would be now. He turned to raise a finger, just in case Luke happened to be looking out.

Mum glanced at him, tutting at his jaunty walk. 'Don't look so pleased with yourself, Hal. This goes on your school record. It's nothing to celebrate. Besides, we've got another problem now.'

Hal looked at her.

'Next week,' Mum said. 'You can't have forgotten? My operation! I'll be in hospital the whole time you're off school.'

He *had* forgotten, sort of. Now he shrugged. ' 'Sall right. I'll be at Osman's.'

'You *were* going to Osman's. Now we'll have to think again. You can't hang around his house on your own while he's at school. Both Osman's parents go out to work.'

'I'll stay in. See Oz in the evenings.'

She shook her head. 'Don't be silly, Hal. You can't spend a week there by yourself.'

'Oz's parents won't mind.'

'Maybe not,' said Mum, 'but *I* mind. I'll phone them tonight and explain. And they might just think you're a bad influence on Osman – he might start getting into trouble too, if he goes around with you and Luke.'

'Nah! He wouldn't, not Oz. So what, then? What're you saying?'

They'd reached the car; Mum shook her head as she got into the driver's seat. 'I don't know. I'll have to work something out.'

He had no idea what she meant by that.

It felt weird going back home halfway through the morning. Hal began to think of the free time stretching ahead, but Mum had other ideas. Instead of going along to

JJ's, she came up to the flat with him. 'We'll divide your time up into subjects, like at school. You can have little breaks, but definitely no TV, no PlayStation.' She fetched paper and a pen, and started drawing up a timetable. 'When I come back I want you to show me what you've done. Looks like your teachers have given you enough to get on with.'

It wasn't going to be a holiday, that was clear.

At first he liked the novelty of having the day to himself, the radio on (Mum hadn't prohibited that) and thinking what lessons they'd be having at school. Very soon, though, it got boring. Do some work. Do a bit more. Slow down. Pretend he was working. Stop even pretending. Send a text to Osman. Get one back. The hours had never passed so slowly. Still, it was the weekend tomorrow, and Mum surely didn't expect him to slog on with the school-work *then*.

She brought in fish and chips for their tea, as she often did on Friday. Afterwards Hal was allowed to have the TV on, and Mum retreated into her room. She was there for a very long time. Crossing the landing to fetch a drink, Hal heard her talking on the phone.

'No, it's not that.' Her voice was quiet; he had to listen very hard. 'I worry about him, Claire, I really do. The fighting, the lashing out . . . what if he gets into *really* bad trouble? Really hurts someone? Mmm . . . mmm . . . I know . . .' Then a few sniffs – maybe she was even *crying*. He stood, mortified; she started again: 'Yes, but . . . All this anger they keep talking about at school! I don't know where it comes from – I never see it. He's such a lovely boy, really he is – well, *you* know . . . Mmm . . .' More sniffs. 'And now next week – no! I'm not asking for special favours, not when . . . I know you would, but there's no way I'd expect . . . No, I can't see any other choice. I'll ring Aunt Jude, ring her now, see if she can take him. He won't like it, but what else can I do? Yes . . . yes, I'll ring you tomorrow night.'

Hal slunk back into the lounge, feeling bad for eavesdropping, bad that Mum was crying because of him. He wished she wouldn't – it wasn't as if he'd turned evil or something, grown vampire teeth or started a career as an axe-murderer. Still, she was making plans for him, plans she hadn't even mentioned; and it sounded like she wanted to farm him out to her Aunt Jude. Aunt Jude! Hal was outraged. He'd only met her a couple of months ago; he hardly knew her. She was Mum's aunt, Hal's *great*-aunt, so she was old or at least oldish, nearly as old as the grandfather. She lived near the sea, but that was the only good thing to be said. She'd seemed friendly at the crematorium, and back at the house afterwards; but *staying* with her! Not if he had any say. She'd disapprove of him for getting into trouble; she'd be strict, and keep him indoors, toiling away at his school-work.

And that house! The big old house that belonged to his grandfather. The grandfather who hadn't wanted anything to do with Mum or Hal, all these years.

Yeah, and that'll work *how*? as Luke would put it.

Although he felt like a little kid, admitting it to himself, Hal didn't want to be separated from Mum, not now. He never had been, for more than a night or two. And now, with her going into hospital – being taken away—

A cold, prickly feeling came over him at the thought of hospital. His one experience of A & E, when he'd sprained his wrist playing in goal, hadn't been too bad;

he'd been treated as a bit of a hero, war-wounded. But sometimes people went into hospitals and didn't come out.

He thought of his grandmother's funeral. It had been a very hot day in August, which made it seem odd that everyone was standing about dressed in black, talking in low voices. Hal had never been to a funeral before and was mildly interested; it seemed like something from TV or a film. And he didn't even know his grandmother, so there was no need to feel sad. What he did know was that she'd gone into hospital for what was meant to be a minor operation, but had died suddenly from heart failure.

Mum was going into hospital for a minor operation. A routine thing. Nothing at all to worry about, she kept telling him; I'll be in and out, soon back on my feet, a little bit of rest and I'll be fine.

Yeah, right. His grandmother had probably said that, the day before she died.

Hal slumped in front of the TV, but couldn't concentrate; instead he went to the window and stood looking out at the street below. He hadn't thought much about Mum's operation – just another complication of the week ahead, no more serious than a dentist appointment – but it now loomed larger in his mind than all his other problems put together. What if she *died* in there – died as suddenly as her mother had, or stayed in hospital, fading and fading like breath on a mirror until she disappeared altogether? How would he manage without her? What if he ended up alone, with no one who cared about him?

He felt as numb and shocked as if it had already happened, so was startled back into the present when Mum walked in. She was smiling, looking relieved.

24

'Hal! I've just been talking to Aunt Jude. She's agreed to help us out. You can go and stay with her for the whole fortnight. She's looking forward to having you.'

'Stay with your dad?' Hal blurted. 'No way.'

'No, my dad's not there. He's gone to Spain for a month. It'll be just you and Aunt Jude.'

Hal opened his mouth with a new protest, but knew that he couldn't.

'Uh,' was all he said.

4
MARBLES

On Sunday they set off for Ryton-on-Sea. Hal and Mum.
Although Mum kept stressing that this wasn't a
holiday, Hal had other ideas. You couldn't be at the
seaside and not feel a little bit holidayish, whatever your
reason for being there.

Ryton-on-Sea had always seemed somehow out of
bounds, though it was near enough to drive down for a
day; Luke often spent weekends there with his dad. Mum
had been born in Ryton and had lived there as a girl, so she
sometimes mentioned it, but only as a distant place that
seemed marooned in the past. Hal had been there only once,
for the funeral. If he and Mum wanted a day at the seaside,
they'd go to Brighton or Bournemouth, never Ryton.

The exclusion zone around the place was because of the
grandparents. Hal knew that much. Mum had no contact
with them; hadn't had anything to do with them for years.
They might as well not exist. If it hadn't been for Aunt
Jude, Mum wouldn't even have known that her mother
had died.

'We had a quarrel, me and my parents,' was all Mum would ever say. 'When I was a student.'

And when Hal asked, 'What about?' she would only reply, 'Oh – we just didn't see eye to eye, that's all. We couldn't get on. Never did, never will.'

So what was the point of going to the funeral, then? Hal didn't get that – but they had gone, all the same. He and Mum went down in the car, Hal feeling dressed up and strange in his school trousers, with a dark jacket and tie borrowed from Claire's son because he didn't have anything suitable. He pictured his grandfather as tall, stern and forbidding. He'd have a beaky nose and bushy eyebrows and little sharp eyes like lasers, and he'd hunch his shoulders when he walked. And he'd always wear black, not just for funerals.

It was a bright, blustery day. At the crematorium, bordered by stunted trees through which the sea could be glimpsed, Hal was led up to a smallish, frail-looking man, with sparse strands of hair and a tanned, freckly face. It was Aunt Jude who introduced them: 'Gerry? Here's Tina – you know I told you she was coming? And here's Hal.'

There was an awkward, startled moment when the man seemed to jump and stare, and then he held out his hand to Mum, and she did the same, as if they were going to shake hands like people at a business meeting. It took Hal a few seconds to realize that this was *him*, Mum's dad, his grandfather. Yes, he *looked* like a grandfather; the sort of grandfather someone else might have.

Instead of shaking Mum's hand, the man took hold of it with both his own, and held tight. 'Christina, Christina. It's been a long time,' he said. 'Far too long.'

No one ever called Mum *Christina*. She was always Tina.

27

'Yes,' was all she said. And then, 'Dad, this is Hal.'

'Hal,' the grandfather repeated, and turned to look at him. He reached out and gripped Hal's hand in a firm, dry clasp. Hal didn't know what to say, so said nothing while the old man looked searchingly into his face. His eyes weren't like lasers after all, but watery and sad. 'My word,' he said. 'You're taller than me already, young man.'

'Hal's been wondering what he should call you,' said Mum.

'Oh . . .' The grandfather gave a wobbly smile. 'Well, my name's Gerry, but you could call me Grandad, couldn't you? Do you think you could manage that?'

He must have thought Hal was about eight years old. And Hal wasn't sure he *could* call him Grandad, so was glad when a vicar came billowing up and told Aunt Jude that it was time to go into the Chapel of Remembrance. Aunt Jude linked her arm through the grandfather's, and nodded to Mum to follow. As they walked into a dimly lit interior like a small church, the grandfather turned to Mum. 'Come back to the house after, you and Hal. You will, won't you?'

Hal didn't get this at all: treating them like long-lost relatives, when they lived less than two hours' drive away. The grandfather hadn't wanted to be friendly for the whole thirteen years of Hal's life; so why now? Hal thought he ought to hate him – especially if what Luke said was true – but while he was wondering whether he did or not, they were inside and there was solemn music playing and the service was beginning. The chapel was far too big for the dozen or so people who came in, mostly quite old, all dressed in black. A few were sniffing into handkerchiefs.

Everyone seemed to know what to do and how to behave – as if there were rules about when to stand and when to kneel, when to talk and when to be quiet and mournful. They knew the tunes of the draggy old hymns, warbling and straining for the high notes, or rumbling away at the deep ones. Hal was ill-at-ease with this God stuff. Mum didn't usually do church either, only for weddings, but she was joining in with the hymns and the Amens. And it was weird, because Hal didn't even know his grandmother, yet his eyes and nose had gone snivelly. He was annoyed with himself; it wasn't as if she was someone he cared about. The coffin was carried in, decked with flowers. There was a real dead body inside, a body that had been alive and a person, but was now a lifeless lump to be burned after the service, reduced to ashes. And it was Mum's mum in there. Awesome, really. But imagine if it were someone he *knew*.

The vicar was talking about someone called Brenda, and it took Hal a few moments to realise that this was his grandmother's name. At the end of the service, curtains opened and the coffin slid through. As he stretched to see, curious about how that worked, Hal heard someone near him give a gulp. Then there was more music, and Aunt Jude and the grandfather led the other guests slowly down the aisle and outside. In the dazzle of sunshine, Hal saw that the grandfather looked weepy and sort of shrunken. Aunt Jude seemed to be holding him up.

Afterwards, back at the grandfather's house, people were more cheerful; there was conversation and even some laughing. There were little sandwiches and sausage rolls and iced cakes, and it was a bit like a party. Now the guests were interested in Hal.

'And this must be—?'

'*Oh*, so you're Christina, and is this your son? Gerry and Brenda's grandson?'

'Oh! I didn't realise . . .'

No one referred to the fact that Mum hadn't spoken to her parents or set foot in this house for more than thirteen years. But it was one of those times when Hal was conscious that he didn't look like Mum, and Mum didn't look like him, and people saw them without realising that they belonged together. And no one else had dark skin, no one at all.

If only he had a dad here as well, it would be clear. For want of a father of his own, he pictured Osman's, with his glossy dark skin and his brilliant smile and his comfortable manner. Osman was so lucky that sometimes Hal almost hated him. Apart from being liked by nearly everyone, Oz had a proper family and a nice house full of laughter and music and welcome, and a big brother who worked in a record shop. Most of all he had a dad. So did Luke, only Luke's dad didn't live at home and of course he wasn't black. So it was Osman's dad who Hal pictured now, standing polite and smiling in his best suit.

Yes, that's my mum, and that's my dad. Hal wondered what it would feel like to be able to say that.

Now, soon after their first sighting of the sea – cloud-grey it looked now, not sparkling and enticing as it had been on the day of the funeral – they were on the edge of Ryton, heading towards the centre.

'That's my old primary school,' Mum told Hal. 'So tiny, it seems now!'

He saw red tiles, a window decorated with infant artwork, a playground and car park. It looked small and old compared to the primary school Hal had attended.

'Did you like school?' he asked her.

'Mm, I did,' said Mum. 'Can you picture me, skipping along the road in my gingham dress and sandals, with my satchel and my lunch-box and my hair in two plaits?'

Hal couldn't really imagine Mum as any different from the way she was now: always neatly dressed, with hair styled and highlighted, and careful make-up. She had to have properly done hair, of course, or people wouldn't trust her with theirs.

She turned left along the sea-front, or what she called the *promenade*. The road ran alongside a pebble beach, with banks of shingle reaching up to the road. The tide was low, and a few people were walking on smooth sand near the water's edge, throwing sticks for dogs or huddling into their coats. Sturdy barriers of blackened wood, which Mum said were called groynes, marched down into the sea. The other side of the wide street was lined with shops and bed and breakfast places, an amusement arcade, a fish-and-chip shop, a newsagent's with stands of postcards outside.

'Oh, the beaches here are so lovely,' Mum said. 'You'll like exploring. Wonderful sand, at low tide. Wonderful sea, wonderful sky. It makes me realise how I miss it.'

'Must have been cool, living at the seaside.'

'Yes. Yes, it was. Oh, look, Hal – there's Marborough's, with the FOR SALE signs all over it. It's sad to see it shut up like that.'

31

It was his grandparents' business, Hal knew, which they'd owned for years and years; Mum had driven him past, to show him, when they came down for the funeral. 'It was quite old-fashioned – the sort of place you could buy golf clubs or a wedding hat or wool for knitting,' she'd told him. 'The top floor was toys and games, and there was a sports department, and luggage, and sewing stuff – oh, all sorts of things. But it's hard for that kind of shop to survive, these days.'

Hal saw the name MARBOROUGH'S DEPARTMENT STORE in gold letters above the revolving doors. Weird, seeing his own name on a shop-front. He'd thought that before and he thought it now.

'What a shame.' They'd stopped at red traffic lights; Mum turned to look at the blank windows. 'It was always part of Ryton, Marborough's was. I wonder what'll happen to it now?'

'Is he rich then, your dad?' Hal asked.

'No – not really. Well, richer than us, but that's not saying much, is it? The shop was making a loss, towards the end. He'll get the money from the sale, but he'll probably invest it. Aunt Jude's taking care of the finances. She's an accountant.'

'Does she always live with him, then? Is it her house as well?'

'No, she's worked abroad for years and years – in Portugal, then in France. She's back to stay now, and she's bought herself a flat, but she hasn't moved in yet. She's looking after my dad's house, while he's away.'

Hal's grandfather was in Spain, visiting a friend who lived there. According to Aunt Jude, he'd always been meaning to go, but the grandmother wouldn't fly, and it was too far to drive. Now he'd gone by himself, for a break. Hal was glad he wouldn't be there. How could he have stayed with the man who'd been horrible to Mum? Aunt Jude, formidable though she looked, wasn't *that* bad. Hal hadn't spoken to her much, but he had the impression that she was in charge; that the grandfather couldn't have managed without her, at the funeral or when people came round afterwards.

'I always got on well with Aunt Jude,' Mum told him. 'She used to stick up for me.'

'About what?'

She put on her vague look. 'Oh — you know – whenever there was trouble.'

'School trouble?' Hal said, thinking of his own.

'No – I was never really in trouble at school. I mean, well, just family stuff.'

'Were they strict, then, your mum and dad?'

'You could say that. In some ways they were.'

'And what about her? Aunt Jude?'

Mum laughed. 'Oh, she'll keep you in order, all right. It's not a holiday, like I said.'

Still, she'd mentioned the beaches, and exploring. Aunt Jude wasn't going to keep him shut indoors the whole time, was she? If she tried, he could always escape.

They turned away from the sea-front now, into a quiet road of houses set well back from the street. The gardens each side were bright with berries and autumn leaves; some even had palm trees and spiky plants that gave an exotic, seaside look. It was very different from the road they lived in at home, which was always lined both sides with cars and vans, every parking space hotly contested. Mum turned left again into a cul-de-sac. Hal recognised

33

the house now, at the far end. It had its own driveway and garage, and was sheltered from the road by a high hedge.

Mum pulled into the driveway and parked. Only now did it occur to Hal that this was the last time he'd have her to himself.

'You, uh – will you be all right next week?' he faltered. 'In hospital, I mean?'

Unfastening her seatbelt, she leaned across and hugged him. 'Yes, Hal. It'll be fine, really it will. Don't you worry about me. I'll phone as soon as I can.'

Reluctantly he got out of the car and went to the boot for his holdall. The road was so quiet. It wasn't going to be much fun, stranded here. For *two whole weeks*. Away from Mum, away from his friends, away from everything he knew.

Aunt Jude came to the door, and kissed both Mum and Hal. At the funeral she'd been smartly dressed in a black jacket and skirt, but today she looked more casual in a bright red sweater and khaki jeans. She'd invited Mum and Hal to lunch; warm delicious smells drifted out to the hall, and music played from the kitchen. With no grandfather at home, and no funeral guests, the house felt different – brighter, airier.

'I'll show you your room first,' Aunt Jude told Hal, after the usual grown-up remarks had been exchanged about the weather and the journey. 'It's your mum's old one.'

Having been so anxious to get here on time, Mum now seemed reluctant. Carrying Hal's rucksack, she followed Aunt Jude up the stairs, with Hal behind. The house was spacious: wide staircase, high ceilings. There were paintings on the walls, and an open door showed him a bathroom with an expanse of black-and-white floor tiles. Hal's – Mum's – room was at the back of the house, looking over the big garden. Besides the bed, wardrobe and bedside cabinet there was a washbasin, a desk with bookshelves above, and a hinged reading lamp.

'It's weird, being back in my own room.' Mum moved around, looking at everything. 'It's been redecorated. I had turquoise wallpaper, and posters everywhere. Sting and the Police – I was mad about Sting.'

'Still are.' Hal pulled a face.

Mum smiled, and said, 'I remember being told off for making Blu-Tack marks on the walls, and having my music too loud.'

'I know – seems like yesterday,' said Aunt Jude. 'There's plenty of room for all your things, Hal. This is empty, look.' She opened both doors of the wardrobe, showing a hanging rail one side and shelves the other.

'I almost expected to see all my old clothes in there,' Mum said.

'It was full of Brenda's things, till last week,' Aunt Jude told her. 'I've just had a big clear-out to the charity shop. Thought I'd do it while Gerry was away – I asked him first, of course. Anyway, Tina, do you want to help Hal unpack and settle in? Lunch in about twenty minutes.' She left them to it.

'It's so lovely and quiet here.' Mum began to take things out of the holdall, hanging clothes in the wardrobe or putting them folded on shelves. 'That's what I remember. Hearing birds in the garden, and the gulls. Always the gulls.'

Too quiet, Hal thought. It'd be like prison. What was he meant to do here, with no TV in his room, no computer?

What if there was no computer in the whole house, no wireless broadband?

'Mum, what am I—' he began.

She'd stopped unpacking, her eyes fixed on something in the holdall. She lifted out the bag of marbles and held them up.

'What—' She glanced at him, then opened the draw-string and looked inside. 'I had no idea you still had these! After all this time! What are they doing in your bag?'

He felt his face going hot. 'I put them in. Don't know why.'

Mum smiled, and said lightly, 'I suppose Aunt Jude might give you a game of marbles.'

Hal shrugged, as if they were just toys. As if they'd got into his bag by mistake.

5
TWITCHY

'Come on in,' said Aunt Jude, down in the kitchen, 'and meet Don.'

Hal hadn't realised there was another person in the house. Neither, to judge from her look of surprise, had Mum. A man stood at the sink, washing lettuce: a thin, wiry man with grey hair pulled back into a pony-tail.

'My niece Tina, and my great-nephew Hal,' Aunt Jude told him.

'Know that, don't I?' said the man. 'Saw them at the funeral.'

'Yes, but I didn't introduce you properly then,' Aunt Jude said, lifting her chin. 'You were being curmudgeonly. This is Don, Don Inchbold. He's my lodger,' she explained to Hal and Mum.

'Pleased to meet you,' said Mum.

The man didn't shake hands, just said something like, 'Nnng,' and gave a jerk of his head as if his attention was caught by something behind him. Then he flapped a wet lettuce-leaf at Hal by way of greeting.

'Lodger and very good friend,' said Aunt Jude, 'though it's sometimes hard to tell.'

Hal stared at the man with interest. He must be quite old, but his grin was cheeky and boyish. He wore a navy fisherman's smock with smears of paint on it, and baggy cut-offs that reached just below his knees, with thin brown legs showing beneath. On his feet were plimsolls without laces, and odd socks – one red, one blue.

Mum frowned. 'Don Inchbold? I thought I knew your name when I heard it before, but I still can't think why.'

'He's an artist,' said Aunt Jude. 'Quite a famous one, back in the sixties.'

Don made a tutting sound. 'Don't start on about that. They're not interested in ancient history, are they?'

'They might be!' Aunt Jude moved over to the shelves and took down a bottle of olive oil, but Don elbowed her aside.

'Give me that,' he told her. 'I'll do it. You can't rush the making of a good dressing.'

'I *have* heard of you,' Mum told him; 'I knew it. I'll do an internet search.'

'Kuh!' Don's face seemed to contort; he made an impatient movement with one shoulder and arm. 'Don't waste your time. Load of old tat, I was turning out back then.'

Hal saw Mum's look of startled uncertainty; she didn't know how to take this blunt-speaking, twitchy man. Was Don being rude, or just making fun of himself? And did he actually *live* here, if he was the lodger?

'It wasn't tat! You're the only one that thinks so,' Aunt Jude told him. 'Sit down, you two, and let me fetch you a drink. We'll be all day, this rate.'

Hal's grandfather had a special dining room, with shiny

striped wallpaper and polished furniture; the food had been in there last time, all prissy, with flowered plates and napkins and sandwiches with their crusts cut off. Today they ate in the kitchen, which was much nicer: a jar of bright leaves and berries on the windowsill, no cloth on the table, and the various sections of the Sunday paper to be cleared out of the way. The food was good, too, when it came – lasagne, cheesy-topped, hot and runny with tomato sauce; herb bread, and salad with the tangy dressing Don had made.

'Are you lodging *here*?' Mum asked Don.

He gave one of his funny jolts, accidentally tossing a piece of lettuce from his fork across the table; he reached for it with his fingers and put it into his mouth. 'Lord, no,' he said, crunching. 'Me and her on top of each other all the time? We'd drive each other demented. No, I'm staying in the flat.'

'*My* flat, that is, the one I've bought for myself, in Holly Drive,' Aunt Jude explained. 'I don't need it while I'm here. Soon as I do, I'll turf him out.'

'She would, too,' said Don, helping himself to more lasagne. 'Out on the streets with just the clothes I stand up in. Doesn't mess about, Jude doesn't.'

'Hal, have some more while it's still going.' Aunt Jude passed the dish. 'He might as *well* live here. Always turns up at mealtimes expecting to be fed.'

'Someone's got to show you how to cook a decent meal.' Don stopped chewing and looked straight at Hal, his small blue eyes peering from beneath bristly eyebrows. 'You haven't got much to say for yourself, have you?'

'Uh,' went Hal. It was hard to know how to respond when people said that.

'Give the poor boy a chance,' said Aunt Jude. 'He's only just met you. You take a bit of getting used to.'

'In trouble at school, are you?' Don went on. 'Got yourself chucked out? What did you do, then? Get caught smoking? Call the headmaster a stupid prat? Set off the fire alarm? I did all those when I was at school.'

Hal looked down at his plate.

'No, you see—' Mum began.

'Now don't start giving Hal ideas,' Aunt Jude told Don. 'He needs to put all that behind him. He doesn't need you encouraging him, silly old fool.'

Hal glanced at Mum and saw her expression, surprised and perhaps a little offended by the way Don and Aunt Jude talked to each other. Hal thought they were funny.

And Don, now, had forgotten his question. 'Rules, rules, rules, that's all school was,' he said, waving a piece of herb bread. 'Never learned anything useful till after I left. Rules were only for breaking, that was my view.'

'*Now* who's talking about ancient history?' Aunt Jude looked down her nose at him. 'Schools have changed a bit since your day. Anyway, try talking a bit of sense for once. I'm not having you lead Hal astray.'

Don gave Hal a sidelong look and a conspiratorial chuckle. He must be around the grandfather's age, but he was like a naughty boy. Something odd had happened to Mum, too. She'd gone quiet and sort of girlish, as if the return to her old house had turned her back into the teenager who'd lived here years ago.

And when she left, soon after lunch, Hal felt that he'd shrunk, too, slipped back a few years. Mum kissed and hugged him, reminded him to behave well for Aunt Jude and not to worry, then got into the driving-seat and fastened her seat-belt and sat looking at him. Almost, for a moment, she looked tearful.

'Bye, Prince Hal,' she said, very quietly, using her special name for him. 'Bye, Aunty – thanks again for everything. Goodbye, Don.'

Hal stood on the pavement watching the blue Fiesta turn the corner and out of sight, and suddenly felt more alone than ever in his life. Mum had promised to phone as soon as she could; but first she had to get to the other side of the operation, which now seemed to Hal like a dangerous voyage. They'd put her to sleep and she'd sail into oblivion, while people did things to her. It'd be like *Casualty*. He pictured her lying unconscious on an operating table, masked surgeons bending over her and muttering to each other. Cutting her open.

Mum had laughed when Hal asked her about that. 'Oh, it's very high-tech these days, Hal. They only make a tiny incision. I'm not going to be left like Frankenstein's monster, with great bodged-up scars. I won't know a thing, and I'll be out of there in no time.'

But – what if it went wrong? What if her heart stopped? What if she never woke up? Things like that did happen: it was no good saying they didn't. Not when his grandmother had died that way.

Reluctantly, he followed Aunt Jude indoors. There was lots of the day still left, and the two weeks stretched ahead like blank pages in a diary. OK, the week of school exclusion – he could put up with that. But half-term week as well! He hadn't really made plans, but he'd have gone to football coaching with Osman (not Luke). Probably meet up with a few other mates (not Luke) and hang out in town, or at the sports centre. But here, where he didn't know anyone – what was he meant to *do*? He'd probably die of boredom, and never make it back home.

'Don generally has a snooze after lunch,' Aunt Jude told him. 'Working, he calls it. And I've got to clear up in the kitchen. Why don't you have a look round the garden? When I'm done, we'll walk down to the sea-front and you can start to get your bearings.'

Hal wandered outside. The back garden sloped upwards and was quite large, bordered by trees and shrubs. The leaves and the grass dazzled, autumn-bright. It was an over-tidy sort of garden, with the lawn mown and severely edged, not a weed in sight. Hooped iron bordered the beds of roses and other prim flowers whose names Mum would know. There was a small greenhouse with more plants in it, a stepping-stone path and a pond covered over with netting. Hal couldn't imagine being allowed to kick a football about, or pitch a tent. Course, this was the grandfather's place, and he'd be the kind of old man who spent hours fussing round his garden, picking dead heads off flowers, removing snails, sweeping up leaves. He'd be quick to tell Hal off for breaking stalks or smashing a football into the greenhouse.

Hal hated him. His jaw clenched tight as he thought of what Luke had said. Smashing a football into the greenhouse was exactly what he felt like doing – if only he'd had one.

The house looked so big, so pleased with itself; its back door standing open, its diamond-paned windows, and a flame-coloured creeper climbing to the gutter. Hal felt wrong to be here, even if the old man himself was safely in Spain. It was only Aunt Jude who made it welcoming. The grandfather had tried to be friendly at the funeral, but it was too late now to make up for what he'd done before.

'He's racist,' Luke had said, that Thursday, as they crossed the quad towards the Humanities block. Hal couldn't remember now why they'd started on about the grandfather in the first place – it was somehow triggered by the book they were reading in English – but Luke's speciality was probing where it hurt. 'It's a no-brainer! That's why he chucked your mum out. He couldn't stand the thought of her – you know! – *doing* it, with a black guy. With your dad.'

'Shut *up*!' Hal flung back.

' 'S true though. It's got to be! Why don't you ask your mum?'

Hal hadn't, because he knew it must be true and didn't want to hear her say it. The grandfather had thrown his mother out – hadn't spoken to her for more than thirteen years. Because of Hal.

How was he meant to feel about that?

It got worse. Hal started saying things about Luke's mum, the number of boyfriends she'd had. Below the belt, that was, because Luke had taken a big dislike to his mum's latest, a big bloke with a bullying air who'd started staying over at weekends. And in return, Luke said that Hal's mum was obviously a lezzie because she never had any boy-friends at all.

'Course she's not!' Hal retorted.

Osman gave a theatrical sigh. 'For God's sake, you two! Leave it!'

'Prove it, then. Go on,' Luke taunted Hal.

'Right, well, for one, there's *me*. *I'm* evidence, aren't I?

43

Unless you're even thicker than you look. Two, she *has* had a boyfriend. Dave, last year.'

That had shut Luke up, temporarily. Osman shouldered his way between them and headed off towards the Humanities corridor. Which was where hostilities broke out all over again.

Now, snapping the head off a smug red daisy-flower, Hal crushed it in his hand and let the scarlet petals flutter to the grass. Then he dropped what was left of the flower's centre, and mashed it to pulp with his trainer. It was a pathetic little gesture, but somehow satisfying. He glanced up at the house windows to see if anyone was watching, but no one was.

He didn't want his mum to have boyfriends. When she'd been going out, briefly, with Dave – divorced, forty, kids of his own – Hal had fretted that they'd all move in together and everything would change. Then there'd been a time when Claire had tried to pair Mum up with a friend of a friend. Luckily Mum had decided he was the most boring man she'd ever met.

They were OK as they were, him and Mum. But now he was stuck with family he didn't want, forced to live in the grandfather's house. The home of the person he disliked – despised – more than anyone in the world.

The grandfather didn't want him to exist. Hadn't wanted him to be born. Preferred to cut his own daughter out of his life than to let Hal in.

6
TIDE

'You can't work all day long,' Aunt Jude told Hal at breakfast, as if that was his declared intention. 'If you do a stint this morning, you might like to go out later and see what Don's up to. Looks like being a nice day.'

Don arrived while they were finishing their toast, though he didn't want anything to eat, only strong coffee. It seemed that he usually stopped off here on the way down to the beach hut where he did his painting.

'Kuh! Wants you to check up on me,' Don told Hal, with one of his uncontrolled jerks. 'That's what she's after. Sticking her nose in.' Coffee sloshed over his trousers from the mug he was holding. It must have been hot, but he didn't seem bothered; just wiped at it with his hand.

'Nonsense.' Aunt Jude tore a sheet of kitchen towel from the roll, and dabbed at him. 'I'll be too busy, as well you know. Hal, my mobile number's on the board there. I've got a meeting at the solicitor's that'll take up most of the morning. But I should be finished by lunchtime. Try not to worry about your mum – she'll be fine, really she will.

We'll phone the hospital at tea-time. It'll all be over by then.'

'What's this, then? Hospital?' Don said sharply. 'No one told me anything about hospital.'

Aunt Jude gave an exaggerated sigh. 'Course I did! More than once. Why don't you try *listening*? It's the main reason Hal's here: Tina's operation.'

'What? I thought he'd got himself chucked out of school and that was why.'

'Oh, dear. Take no notice, Hal. Don't know why I waste my breath.'

'Hospital, you'd never get me near the place.' Don reached for the toast-crust Aunt Jude had left on her plate, and crammed it into his mouth. 'If you're not ill when you go in, you will be when you come out,' he said, chewing. 'I'd rather take my chances.'

'Only because you've never *been* really ill,' Aunt Jude snapped at him. 'What a thing to say, today of all days! Don't listen,' she added to Hal. 'He hasn't got the sense he was born with.'

'Kuh!' went Don, with a great shoulder-spasm, and turned aside in his chair as if he couldn't bear to look at her.

Hal couldn't work them out. Why was Don always round here, if they were so impatient with each other? And he wanted to know why Don did all that twitching and jerking, but couldn't come straight out and ask.

Before she left, Aunt Jude installed Hal in the dining room with his maths books. Don made a round of sandwiches, humming tunelessly all the while, then he looked in at Hal, said 'Rather you than me,' and let himself out, carrying his lunch in a frayed canvas shoulder-bag. Hal felt envious. Yesterday afternoon, out on their walk, they'd passed the beach huts, and Don had said that Hal could go down there whenever he liked.

Now would be good, Hal thought. Better than sitting here with nothing to save him from his linear equations. It felt weird being left alone in the house. Silence and loneliness settled around him like dust.

The dining room wasn't a good place to be. Unlike the kitchen, which Jude had taken over with her own things and her cooking smells, and the cork board with postcards and Post-Its stuck all over, the dining room was a cold and formal place, in which he could only think of his grandfather. Not the stooped, tearful man he'd seen at the crematorium, but the grandfather of his imagination, the one who'd thrown Mum out of the house. Had it really been as drastic as that? Had he ordered her to pack her bags and leave? Even physically bundled her out onto the doorstep?

All because he'd taken against Hal's father. If what Luke said was right.

Mum.

On the wall was a square-faced clock of dark polished wood, ticking away, emphasising the house's emptiness. She'd be at the hospital now, for tests and stuff, though her operation wasn't till this afternoon. Two o'clock, she'd been told, so he must remember to think about her then. Things might go wrong if he failed to do that.

His maths textbook was open in front of him, with the printed sheet of instructions sent by Mr Khalid, but his brain was reluctant to confront the exercises. The numbers and words might have been in secret code, for all the sense they made. Compared to this, school would be fun – the group work, the experiments and the cooking, the art and drama, the joyful release of PE, the kickabouts at lunch-time, the jokes and the laughing. He'd never expected to miss school, but now he did. If only he could have school without the trouble that seemed intent on tripping him up, like a dog getting under his feet.

He picked up his pen, put it down again, began to feel so annoyed with the *tock-tock-tock*ing of the clock that he could have tugged it down from the wall and stamped on its stupid face.

'I hate you.' He was speaking to his grandfather, and his words shocked him with their loudness, seeming to bounce back at him off the walls. 'I hope you drop down dead in Spain and never come back.'

Someone would know what he'd said. His words would re-echo later, and someone would hear them, and know. Edgily he looked around him, at the plum velvet curtains with their tasselled tie-backs, at the display cabinet full of china. He didn't belong here. Wasn't wanted. Everything in this over-neat, over-clean, over-silent room seemed to tell him so.

He had to get out. If he stayed here he'd have to smash something. He slammed his maths book shut and thrust his chair back from the table.

Aunt Jude had shown him the spare door-key, on a row of hooks near the back door, where old coats hung. Underneath, by the mat, stood walking boots and green wellies. Presuming the wellingtons were his grandfather's, Hal kicked them over; they sagged sideways, green and limp.

He could get back before Aunt Jude did. She needn't know; she could think he'd been doing what he was told, slogging away at his maths. He didn't fancy getting on the wrong side of her; the set of her mouth and the keenness of her stare told him she could be stern if things didn't go as she expected.

But, for now, he'd escaped. He felt a great sense of freedom as he jogged down the cul-de-sac and turned right into Laurel Drive, wider and tree-lined. It was cooler than he'd thought, the air carrying the unmistakable salty lure of the sea, and the cry of gulls. He broke into a run, feeling how his legs wanted to stretch and be strong, his feet carrying him fast down the road. A woman lifting shopping bags from a car boot gave him a curious look, probably wondering why he wasn't safely locked up in school, on a Monday in term-time. Hal ignored her, his trainers pounding the pavement as he sprinted past.

He had to get to the sea.

At the main road, traffic signs pointed to Brighton one way, Chichester and Town Centre the other. Now he could see, over the roofs of bungalows in the street below, the huge stretch of sea, blue-grey, endless. Sunlight and cloud-shadow made its surface change and shimmer. Far out, a bar of golden light lay on the horizon.

Across the road, a gravelly footpath led between two bungalows and down to the sea-front. This was the way they'd come back from their walk yesterday afternoon, Hal, Aunt Jude and Don. Don's beach hut was along to the left, beyond the edge of the town, with rough grass and windblown trees behind. Hal was curious about Don, alone there and apparently quite happy with that, but now he wanted the sea to himself. The gulls' screaming was loud and insistent: sometimes a drawn-out wail, sometimes a shrill repetition, that seemed to promise excitement not far away.

He'd reached the coast road, the road Mum and Aunt Jude called the promenade. When the tide was at its highest, Aunt Jude said, waves had been known to rear up high, flooding the road. The tide now was halfway in, or halfway out: Hal couldn't tell which, but then remembered that Don had said something about swimming at high tide later, so it must be coming in. Swimming! He must be a tough old boy. Hal had sometimes swum in the sea, but only in hot summer weather, not like this when wind gusted through the gaps in his clothing. And the sea looked so cold and vast, not bobbing with heads and coloured balls, lilos and swimming dogs, as on those summer beach days.

Stones clinked and grated beneath his feet. Here, the power of the waves had made banks of shingle. At high tide, Mum had told him, the beach was all pebbles. He could see where the latest tide had reached, marked by clumps of red-brown seaweed, and a discarded plastic spade, bright blue. Below, the shingle gave way to firm sand, streaked with runs of smaller stones. Further still, smoothed by retreating waves, the sand was flattened and firm, with runnels and ripples and occasional small pools hollowed by the tide where a rock was lodged.

Hal walked. Under his feet the grate and grind gave way to the crunch of gritty sand, then to ribbed firmness. Each footprint pressed out water, then quickly filled. Looking behind him, he saw his tracks following, large sure footprints that could have belonged to someone who knew where he was going.

When he stood at the very edge of the sea, where the water was no more than a film, he watched how the tiniest waves lifted and surged, then fell back ready for the next push forward, leaving sandy bubbles. After only a few moments he had to pull his feet free and move inshore, or he'd be up to his ankles.

It was because of the moon, he knew that. They'd done it in science. But he didn't really understand how the moon pulled and made tides. Without the moon, all the water of the sea would just lie there. There'd be no waves, no surfing, no high and low tide. No sound. The sea was calm today, but still there was wave-sound: just the lift and wash, ripple and fall. It became part of his thoughts, regular, almost hypnotic. Its rhythm seemed part of his mind. Part of the blood pumping through him to his own heartbeat.

He thought about wading into the sea, just as he was, in all his clothes. Perhaps he'd find he could breathe underwater, grow a fish's tail, strong and muscular. He'd swim and swim and never come up for air.

Just a thought. A stupid one. It wouldn't be like that. But what if he just floated into the water, let it carry him away? Is that how it would be for Mum, having the anaesthetic? Where would she go? How would she get back?

He wished Osman could be here – good old Oz, always easy, very rarely in a mood. Even Luke would be better than no one. They could find a little stream to dam, make a fire, search the tideline for stuff washed up. He didn't feel like doing much on his own.

Maybe he'd go along to Don's after all. Just walk past, look in.

He began to wander along in the direction of the beach huts. There was a row of wooden chalets, painted blue with yellow doors and window-frames, neat and simple as children's drawings. Don's, next to them, was more of a cabin, flat-roofed, with a ramshackle verandah on stilts, and steps up. The proper beach huts were locked up, but Don's door stood open, with a wicker chair out on the deck. He'd be inside, painting. He painted every single day, Aunt Jude said; it was the only thing he really liked doing.

Hal slowed, reluctant to face Don, such a strange man, with no one else there. What would he say, and what would Don say back, without Aunt Jude to take charge? Don would *Kuh* at him, would twitch and drop things. He might be cross at being disturbed.

Turning away, Hal saw a flattened piece of wood marooned with the drying seaweed of the tidemark. Tiny flies swarmed up as he reached for it. It was some kind of narrow bat, used perhaps for a beach game and now forgotten or thrown aside. The damp wood had warped at the edges but it still had a tattered rubber grip around its handle.

He didn't know why he wanted it, but was reluctant to sling it back. He whacked it against his hand, then looked round in case there was a ball to be found as well. That was too much to hope for. Instead, he went down alongside the groyne to the sand, and tried using the bat as a flat spade to dig with.

There was a satisfying gritty crunch as he pushed in, and scooped. The sand had just the right degree of dampness; each slice-mark stayed clean and firm as he dug. At first he just heaped at random, but then he realised how well the sand could be moulded and shaped. With sweeps and slaps of the bat, he began to sculpt.

If anyone saw him, they'd think he was like a little kid, making sand-pies. But he wasn't. He was thinking on a larger scale. He'd make a whale, perhaps – a killer whale. He'd seen them on TV; seen them thrusting through the water, sleek and sure, boldly black and white, streamlined as fighter aircraft. A sand whale would be washed away when the tide came in, but that wouldn't matter. He dug and smoothed, patted and shaped, stood back and looked. But to make even a roughly-shaped killer whale, life-size as he wanted, would take more time than he had, with the tide coming in – already the waves had edged closer. To do it properly he'd need to work out the best time: start while the tide was on its way out.

Only now did he notice two people watching him.

One was a skinny kid, a boy in a red hoodie and a black knitted hat. He stood on the shingle-bank with his fists pressed hard into the hoodie's pockets, the zip drawn right up to his chin. How long had he been there? When he saw Hal staring, he turned and walked off towards the town. Not particularly hurried, not so that it looked as if Hal had seen him off; just as if he'd been going in that direction anyway.

The other watcher was Don. He'd come out of his hut and was standing at the top of a short flight of wooden steps that led down to the shingle.

'Hal!' he yelled. 'Hal!'

Hal felt himself snatched back from wherever he'd been. He seemed to have worked on the sand-sculpture for several hours, though of course it couldn't have been that long, or the tide would be fully in. But it had taken up his thoughts and actions in a way that – now he'd been jolted out of it – felt good, felt urgent and real. Now he remembered Mum, waiting in hospital, while he'd let her slip right out of his thoughts. And he was meant to be back in his grandfather's dining room doing equations, waiting for Aunt Jude to come back from wherever she'd been. Irritation surged back, tugged at him.

He wasn't doing anything wrong, so why was Don shouting?

Getting no reply, Don stood for a few moments longer, then gave up and went back inside.

Hal was colder than he'd realised. He licked at the damp saltiness on his lips, felt a shiver around his neck and his middle, and his face filmed with sea-damp.

He plodded over the pebbles to see what Don wanted. He thought of chucking the old wooden bat aside, but then didn't, and took it with him. When he turned to look back at the half-formed whale, part of him was sorry to leave it, but another part said that he might as well stop wasting his time. Nothing he ever did turned out the way he wanted.

7

FAMOUS

For a moment, his steps slowing, Hal thought Don had called him over to tell him off, for playing about on the beach instead of staying indoors. But how likely was that? Don didn't sound like he could care less about school or rules.

Hal stepped inside the hut.

'I'm having a brew-up,' Don said. 'Coffee?'

'Uh, yeah, go on then.'

The hut was bigger than it looked from outside and smelled pungently of tar and spirit and coffee. It was well-lit through a skylight in the roof. An easel was set up, facing away from Hal, next to an old table spattered with paint and littered with jam jars, bits of paper and squeezed-out tubes. There was a battered sofa with a fringed blanket thrown over it, another wicker chair and a shelf of art books. Canvases on frames rested against one wall; the other was stuck all over with pencil and ink sketches and scribbled notes.

On a little fold-up table at the back Don had a camping-stove with a kettle perched on top. Flames flickered blue, and the kettle let out a piercing whistle. Don turned off the gas, poured steaming water into two mugs, and stirred vigorously.

'There.' He handed one to Hal, and motioned him to sit on the sofa. 'This'll warm you up.'

Hal sat. Fine grains of sand glinted on the floorboards and in the red-and-turquoise pattern of the rug. From the sofa he could look straight out at the sea. Don sat on the stool by his easel. He wore fingerless gloves, and a black fringed scarf tied under his chin, and a padded waistcoat with pencils and crayons sticking out of the pockets.

'Saw you down there,' he said. 'Kuh. Looked like you were having fun.'

'Uh. Is there—' Hal hadn't meant to ask directly, but now it seemed he was going to '—something wrong with you? I mean, you know.' He found himself mimicking – thrusting out an elbow, jerking his head, doing the *kkk* and the *nnng*.

Don looked at him. 'Oh, that? I'm so used to it I hardly notice any more. Yeah, it's got a name, Something-or-Other Syndrome. Fancy name for being a bit twitchy. Heard of it? I only do the twitching. With some people it makes them shout out rude words. I don't do that – well, I do sometimes, but not because of the How-d'you-call-it.' He gave a mischievous smile, looking for a second like a boy younger and naughtier than Hal.

'There's a boy at school does it,' Hal said. 'The calling out, I mean. Aren't there pills or something?'

'Oh yes, there's pills,' Don answered. 'If I want pills I can have pills. There's always pills.'

Hal wasn't sure what he meant by that. He took a swig of coffee. It was stronger and darker than he liked, almost bitter. He noticed that Don had pulled the easel back so that there was even less chance of seeing the painting propped on it.

'I can take the pills, or I can paint,' said Don. 'Can't do both, and I'd rather paint. What was that you were making?'

Hal shrugged. 'Dunno. Nothing.'

'Didn't look like nothing, the way you were concentrating.'

'Just mucking about.'

'It's good sand for sculpting.' Don stirred his coffee again, then sucked the teaspoon. 'There used to be a chap came here and worked all day, made the most marvellous figures. Neptune, mermaids, sea-serpents. People took photos, but he – nnng – never did. Said the whole point of it was they'd be washed away when the tide came in and there'd be nothing left to show they'd ever been there.'

Don got up and found half a packet of biscuits – gingernuts, gone a bit soggy – and they ate one each.

'Prince Hal, your Mum calls you,' Don remarked.

'Uh.' Hal was embarrassed. No one else was meant to hear. 'And it's Marbles at school.'

'Prince Hal's good though,' said Don, taking another biscuit. 'As a lad he got into all sorts of trouble. Then grew up and turned into – nng – Henry the Fifth. Shakespeare's play, I'm talking about. But I expect you know that.'

'Mum told me.' Hal didn't want to say that she called him that because he was as important to her as a prince or a king; that was what he liked to think, anyway. It would sound stupid, even big-headed. Instead, he looked towards Don's easel, and said, 'Don't you get, like, bored, here all day on your own?'

Don looked at him hard. 'No, I don't. I get annoyed with myself, I get cross, I get frustrated, but never bored.'

'What d'you do, then?'

'I paint. And sometimes I just look. Or think. Or swim.'

Hal nodded at the painting. 'Can I see?'

Don's mouth compressed as if he was going to say *No, mind your own business,* but then he said, 'If you want,' and turned the easel round to show Hal.

Hal had no idea what to expect, and didn't know anything about art anyway; it was his least favourite subject at school. What Don had on his easel was a canvas that was nearly all grey, with two faint lines across it. The painted bits were of the sea: the top faint line was the horizon, and the lower one was the tide's edge, and in between there was just a suggestion of the movement of waves.

'Cool,' was all Hal could think to say.

'Nnng,' said Don. ' 'Sall right. You don't have to like it or anything. There's nothing to like, yet. I might not like it myself. Probably won't.'

Hal looked again, and saw that what he'd taken at first for dull grey was actually alive with movement; the energetic brush-strokes were the surging power of waves; the colours were sunlight shifting on sea. Faint pencil lines outlined a walking figure, a plump woman, side-on. She looked a bit cartoony, but then she wasn't painted yet.

Hal shuffled his feet. 'Who's she?'

'A woman I saw on the beach one day.'

'Why's she in the picture, then?'

'Kuh. Because she looked like she was seeing the sea for the first time in her life. There she is, so ordinary, but she knows she's looking at something quite – nng – miraculous.'

Hal didn't get that.

'The sea.' Don sounded impatient. 'The sea can make you mad. And the sea can make you sane.'

Hal nodded, as if this made any kind of sense. 'So what's it for?'

'*For?*' Don gave him an amused look. 'I dunno. Does it have to be *for* something?'

'I mean, you know, do you sell them, or what? Are they worth a lot?'

'That's – k – two very different questions. No, I don't sell them. They're not worth a penny, not unless—'

He looked up, annoyed, at the sound of feet on the wooden steps. Someone was standing on the deck, looking in – a youngish, dark-haired woman, well wrapped up in a purple coat, and trousers tucked into black boots. Her eyes flicked to Hal, but she was more interested in Don.

'Please excuse me! It's Mr Inchbold, isn't it – Don Inchbold?' She talked very quickly, breathily. 'I hope you don't mind me coming to find you here, but I just—'

'Kuh!' went Don, sounding as if he minded a lot.

'Oh, this is so amazing!' the woman went on. 'I had to come and see if it was really you. I heard you were living in Ryton – *working* here, so exciting! – and I couldn't believe my luck – I've always been such an admirer,' she added to Hal, as if he'd know what she was talking about.

'Luck, how?' said Don, chin jutting.

'Sorry – I ought to introduce myself.' The woman was inside now, though Don hadn't said to come in. 'I'm Amanda Farman. From the Lifeboat Gallery – I'm one of the directors. You must have seen what's going on at the old lifeboat-house – the new extension?'

Don's face registered nothing.

'Yes, we open on Saturday week,' Amanda Farman continued. 'First of November. It's going to be just thrilling – a modern arts centre, a beautiful gallery space for Ryton at last – really it's long overdue, just what the town needs—'

From what he'd seen so far, Hal would have said that the town needed a multiplex cinema or a skateboarding park, not some poncey art gallery. He looked at Don, who rolled his eyes upwards and let out his breath in a small huff. Amanda Farman didn't even notice, but Hal did, and couldn't help grinning – it was exactly the way Luke signalled boredom in a tedious lesson, or when a teacher was having a go. Hal felt that he and Don were allies against the intruder.

'I was hoping – well, that's why I've come along to see you,' Amanda went on, undeterred. 'Is it dreadfully cheeky to ask if you'd be our special guest for the evening – for the official opening? Someone of your stature in the art world, your importance – it'd give us a tremendous boost – a famous name to bring people to the event – fantastic for publicity, and—'

At last she faltered to a stop, in the face of Don's silence. He picked up a paintbrush, and plucked at a loose hair.

Hal was impressed. So Don really was famous, then? It was hard to believe. Surely famous people had more of a glow about them, more dazzle?

Amanda tried again. 'Perhaps you need time to think about it.' She took a notebook from her shoulder-bag. 'If you give me your address, I'll send you a formal invitation. Your email as well, if you would.' She flipped open the notebook and held a pen poised, looking at Don.

'I don't do email,' he said, his attention still on the

brush, 'and, nnng, you've got my address, obviously. It's here.'

Amanda's eyes swept around the hut's interior. 'Oh, but surely—'

'How did you find me?'

'Oh,' said Amanda, taking this as encouragement, 'one of our local artists has seen you coming and going – told me you'd set up a studio here. So exciting! Such an honour for Ryton! And here you are, actually at work – *may* I, just a tiny peek?'

She moved towards the easel, mouth slightly open, eyes wide. At once Don was on his feet, barring her way. He almost snarled, fixing her with a gaze so ferocious that she stepped back hastily.

'Oh, I'm so sorry.' She gave a little laugh. 'So rude of me – please forgive me. I'm just eaten up with curiosity. A Don Inchbold in the making! It's such a very long time since you've exhibited – I'm dying to see your current work. Of course, if you'd consider loaning one of your paintings for display at the opening I'd be honoured beyond words – utterly thrilled. But – entirely up to you, of course. Well, it's been lovely to meet you, Mr Inchbold, I can't tell you what an enormous pleasure – and—' her gaze swivelled to Hal '—I do apologise again for barging in.' She tucked the notebook into her bag, pulled out a wallet and took out a business card. 'Here are my contact details. Do get in touch if you're interested in following this up. Any time. Any time at all.'

'Come on, Hal,' Don said abruptly. 'I'm – nnngg – locking up.' He grabbed a rolled towel and his canvas bag and marched out, followed by a startled Amanda and then Hal. 'See you later,' he told Hal, locking the door. He didn't put the key in his pocket but pushed it underneath a large stone on the decking. Then he jumped down the steps and strode off along the row of huts, in the opposite direction from the town.

Hal and Amanda watched him go. Then Amanda said brightly, 'Well. Hal, is it? You must be very proud of your grandad.'

She actually thought—

'Yeah,' said Hal, letting himself pretend. 'I am.'

8
SANDMAN

Aunt Jude was annoyed. Back from her meeting, she was closing the garage doors as Hal came down the road. She was smart and severe in her business suit, carrying a black briefcase which she put down in the hall.

'It's not good enough, Hal. I promised your mum you'd get on with your schoolwork, and the very first chance I give you, you scoot off out! Can't I trust you? I'm far too busy to stand over you, making sure you do as you're told.'

Hal said nothing; just waited for her to stop. He felt like he had in Mr Blake's office. Nothing he said would make any difference, so why bother? Then she took off her jacket and hung it over the stairpost, and said in a kinder voice, 'I know you're anxious about your mum, so I won't go on about it, not today. I'll make us some lunch as soon as I've got changed. You can do your work this afternoon.'

There was no getting away from it. They had beans on toast with salad, and then Hal was back in the dining room with the shiny wallpaper and the ticking clock, and Aunt Jude sitting opposite with her laptop. Two o'clock came, and the clock hands seemed to stick there for a very long time after the bongs.

'Two o'clock,' Hal said, in case Aunt Jude hadn't remembered.

'Yes,' she said, understanding. 'She'll be all right, Hal. Really she will.'

One good thing was that Aunt Jude knew lots about maths, being an accountant, and when he got stuck with the equations she showed him how to work them out, making it seem easy. He got the impression she quite liked it, solving problems, or, rather, helping *him* to solve them.

'Your mum was just like you, when she was thirteen,' she told him. 'Always thinking she couldn't do things, then finding out she *could* do them, perfectly well. And ended up going to university. She was a clever girl – course, she still *is* a clever girl – only it took her a long time to believe it.'

Hal thought about this. 'People don't usually go to university to be a hairdresser, do they?'

'No – well, no. That's not what she thought she'd be, back then. But she seems to like it. And being Tina, she'd be good at anything she sets out to do.'

Hal nodded. 'She is. And Jacky calls her Agony Aunt.'

'Agony Aunt?'

'Yeah. People tell her, like, all this stuff, you know, while she does their hair, and she helps them sort things out. Sometimes they come specially to talk to her, that's what Jacky says.'

'Mm, I can see that.' Aunt Jude looked a bit sad. 'She'd be a good listener. Sympathetic. But big problems of her own, she must have had. I wonder who listened to *her*? I just wish – oh, what a waste it's been, this stupid family

64

rift! All these years! I wish I'd been around to have a go at sorting things out. I always got on well with Tina.'

'But how could you—' Hal began.

'Well, no.' Aunt Jude humphed a laugh. 'It's big-headed of me to think I'd have smoothed everything over, with such strong-minded people as your mum and your gran and your grandad. Still, I'd have tried. First I heard, Tina had gone off and no one knew where.'

'It was *his* fault though, wasn't it? He chucked her out!'

Hal was looking straight at Aunt Jude – wouldn't she side with the grandfather? He was her brother, after all – but her gaze shifted away, and she gave a big sigh. 'I don't know the ins and outs of it. But what could be so important as to split up a family?'

Me, Hal answered inside his head. It was *me*. But he didn't say it aloud. Surely Aunt Jude must know that.

'Anyway,' she said, 'I'm glad we're in touch now. That's a start. I know you're worried about your mum's operation, but some good's coming out of it. And it's lovely to have a teenager in the family again. Like a breath of fresh air.'

It took Hal a couple of seconds to realise she meant *him*. She smiled, not needing an answer, and went back to whatever she was doing on the laptop.

Mum, at his age, had maybe sat at this same table, imprisoned by her strict father, with a heap of homework. She'd never told him much about her childhood, presumably because of the rows that came later. The old man couldn't have cared for her at all, or he wouldn't have acted as he did.

Hal couldn't imagine that Mum would ever throw *him* out, no matter what he did, no matter how he disappointed her. She wouldn't, she just wouldn't. It was a fact of his life.

He finished the maths, had a break, then toiled away at geography. At six o'clock Aunt Jude phoned the hospital, and was given the news that Mum was fine, very sleepy after her operation, and would be able to talk on the phone tomorrow.

'There! *That's* good. Now we can relax.' Aunt Jude uncorked a bottle of wine, and took a chilled Coke from the fridge for Hal. 'Where can Don have got to? He's usually here by now. Will be, as soon as I start cooking. He usually likes to take over.'

Only now did Hal remember that Don had gone stomping along the beach, several hours ago.

'He walked off,' he told her. 'He was cross, I think, cos some woman came to his hut.'

'When?' Aunt Jude said sharply. 'What woman?'

'Amanda someone. From a lifeboat gallery.'

'Oh, the new arts centre. Came to his *hut*? What did she want?'

Hal tried to pick out the facts from all the gush. 'She wants him to be, like, a special guest when they open. Because he's so famous. *Is* he?'

'Oh dear, that would have upset him,' Aunt Jude said, more to herself than to Hal. She fetched potatoes, onions and carrots from the vegetable rack and ran water into the sink. 'Yes, you could say he's famous, or was. To people who know about art, anyway. Back in the sixties he was one of the Bright Young Things of British painting. Sold his work for ridiculous sums of money. Most of them went to private collections, but his most famous one, *Moony* it's called, was stolen, never seen again. It was in all the papers at the time.'

Hal didn't get this. 'So why does he act weird when people come and tell him he's cool? You'd think he'd like it.'

'Because that was then and this is now. He's changed his style completely. He doesn't want to be the Don Inchbold who had pictures in smart London galleries and was in the news. He thinks he just happened to be fashionable. What he does now is much better, but he doesn't like anyone seeing it. Set the table, could you, Hal? Knives and forks in that drawer there. He'll roll up before long, the silly old grump.'

It seemed odd to Hal that Don practically lived here with Aunt Jude, when neither had a good word to say for the other.

'Don't you like him?' he asked.

'*Like* him?' Aunt Jude turned to him in surprise. 'Course I do. I love him to bits – he's my dearest, closest friend. Couldn't imagine not having him around.'

Don arrived just as Aunt Jude was serving up the shepherd's pie. No one referred to his lateness, nor to Amanda Farman. Don drank wine and ate hungrily, then cut up a pineapple for them all to share, and made strong coffee. If he'd been annoyed earlier, he was over it now. He told Aunt Jude that he'd had a good day, had been swimming, and painted well, and that he'd enjoyed having Hal to visit.

When they'd finished eating and had cleared up, Don and Aunt Jude settled with their coffee to watch some old film on Sky. Hal checked his text-messages: HOW U DOIN? from Osman. COOL, he texted back. If he could get on line, he'd send an email, saying he'd met someone really famous, and had been down on the beach while Oz and Luke had been in double science.

He hadn't seen a computer anywhere in the house, but when he asked Aunt Jude about internet access she said that he could use her laptop for a while. 'For an hour, say, before bed. As long as you're – you know – sensible about it.'

She let him take it into the dining room. Hal sent the email to Oz, then did a Google search for Don Inchbold.

A whole list of results came up, pages and pages of them.

'Don Inchbold was one of the most innovative painters of the 1960s,' he read, and there was a photograph of a much younger but just about recognisable Don, with long dark hair and sideburns, and a T-shirt with purple star-bursts all over it. 'After attending St Martin's College of Art, he exhibited at the Carnaby Street Gallery and the Hayward, to wide acclaim.' And when Hal scrolled down, there were Don's paintings, with titles like *Dream 9* and *Moony* and *Android*. They were nothing at all like the grey painting Hal had seen at the beach hut, with the cartoony figure. They looked more like photographs, clear and sharp: black sky and stars, orbiting capsules, a close-up of the moon that looked so close he thought he could land on it, like the Apollo astronauts. That one, the caption said, had been stolen after being sold to a private buyer, and never seen since.

Still, it was true. Don *was* famous, even if he didn't want to be.

Hal surfed for a bit, then put the laptop back in its case and returned it to Aunt Jude. 'Thanks, Hal. Bedtime now,' she told him.

Don was sprawled out in an armchair, legs apart, hairy shins showing above odd socks, one of which was frayed and unravelling round the top. Hal couldn't help looking at him with new respect. All those hits!

'See you tomorrow, if you feel like another visit,' Don told him.

Hal went upstairs, his head full of the day. Relief about Mum had allowed all the other impressions to surge forward. The sea, the waves, the shingle and the sand. Don's painting. Don marching off in a strop. The things Aunt Jude had said, and the things Don didn't say.

Hal dreamed that he was back on the beach, digging. The wooden bat was firm in his hand; the lull and fall of the waves was inside his head. And the bat-spade seemed full of its own energy; the figure he wanted to sculpt was taking shape as fast as he could heap the sand. He thought at first it was going to be a whale, sleek and streamlined, but it straightened and narrowed, its fins became arms, its tail divided into legs and feet; it had a distinct, faceless head.

He wanted it to look at him. To see him.

Reaching into his pocket he took out a marble. He held it to the light and saw how the lick of green was suspended in clear glass, like a brushload of bright paint caught there, gleaming. He took a second marble from his pocket, then placed both in the sandman's face.

Now the man had eyes. He looked at Hal. The arms began to move, the legs to bend at the knees; the man planted his feet and sat up.

'Who are you?' he said, although he had no mouth.

'I'm—'

'Who are you?'

'I'm—'

The sandman stared. He didn't really need to be told. He stood and faced Hal, looked him up and down with his marble eyes.

Then he turned away and walked into the sea.

'Dad!' Hal tried to shout, but urgency clogged his throat and stopped the word from escaping. It wasn't a word he'd ever said in his whole life, like that, to a Someone.

The sandman waded into the rushing waves, deeper and deeper until the water closed over the top of his head. A cloud of sand spread under the surface, dissolved into separate glinting particles, settled.

Gone.

9
PRINCE

Hal couldn't at first think where he was. The windows, already a rectangle of bright daylight, were in an unfamiliar place; the walls were farther apart than they should be.

Then he remembered.

The dream had left him groggy and dazed, but was vivid in his mind. The sense of loss tugged at him like an ache.

But the marbles were real. He took out the bag and reached in for one, then held it up. It was the pillar-box red one, not green as in his dream, but he slipped it into his pocket in case it brought luck. Then he reached for a second, and this time it *was* green.

'What's the matter?' Aunt Jude asked him, when he went downstairs. 'Slamming doors, crashing about?'

'Nothing.' He couldn't explain; didn't even know what *was* wrong. He was in a bad mood, that was all.

Aunt Jude looked at him, but said no more.

'Look, what a lovely day,' she remarked instead. 'Warmer

than yesterday.' She'd already opened the double doors of the dining room that led out to the garden.

Don appeared briefly, downed two mugs of strong coffee, and said he'd be in the hut all day if Hal felt like dropping in.

After breakfast Aunt Jude said that she had work to do at home: 'So there's no escape for you *this* time, Sonny Jim. But you can go out after lunch if you work well this morning.' She brought her laptop into the dining room and set Hal up with his English, which involved reading two chapters of a book, then writing a playscript. That wasn't too bad; it would have been more fun making it up with Osman or even Luke, but nevertheless he managed to produce something, and had moved on to geography by the time Aunt Jude said they both deserved a mid-morning break. The radio in the kitchen was playing soft music, so even the clock's tocking wasn't as infuriating as it had been yesterday.

'Nothing's as bad as you think, if you get on with it,' Aunt Jude told him cheerfully. 'It gets done.'

All the while, Hal felt the sea tugging him back to it, like the moon pulling the tides. The crunch of pebbles, the salt-laden wind, the shifting colours of sea and sky – part of him was on the shore, even while he sat staring at a graph of population growth in China.

At last, lunch over, enough work done to earn him some time out of the house, he was free, running down Laurel Drive.

It was the day of the match, he remembered, after school today. Soon they'd all be there in the changing room, out on the pitch, warming up, kicking about, without him. Jason Green in his place – it gave him a pain in his chest, thinking about it. This was just year nine versus year ten, but Hal had played once for the under-sixteens and had done better than he could have dreamed, scoring in the second half. Hicksy had set it up beautifully for him; there was the goal-mouth in front, the goalie with hands outstretched, two defenders wavering, and then Hal's boot had slammed into the ball, sending it into an arc of absolute soaring perfection, floating into the top left corner of the net while the goalie's gloved hands flailed uselessly. The ball was drawn there as if it couldn't possibly have gone anywhere else. That moment of pure singing happiness – it might have been the best moment in his entire life. He'd been afloat on it, his heart swelling like a great balloon of pride, his feet light enough to run a marathon. And then the yells going up from his own team, the slaps and the shoves and the beaming faces, and Hal a hero. Could anything be as good as that, ever?

That goal had won them the match. Hal had looked at his right boot with special respect when he took it off. Stroked it. Would have thanked it if no one had been listening. Magic, that was, sheer magic.

The warmer weather had brought out more people today; an elderly couple down on the beach with two spaniels, someone in shorts and a vest, jogging, and a mother with two little girls, toddlers, collecting shells. Hal looked at this group, because they were the first black people he'd seen since arriving at Ryton. 'Vera!' called the mother. 'Come and see what Grace has found.' She smiled at Hal as he passed. She'd made a sort of camp, sheltered by the groyne, with a blanket and buckets and spades and a book lying face-down, and a chill-bag that must have had a picnic in it. But they'd have to move soon, because the tide was racing in – higher than yesterday, already beyond the point where Hal had started making the whale.

He was annoyed. He wanted the beach to himself, and he wanted a big expanse of sand. And he'd left the spade-bat in Don's hut, but he didn't want to go and explain why he needed it.

Remembering the plastic spade he'd seen washed up, he wondered if he might find something else he could use. A bit of old wood might do. While he was looking for that, he found an odd flip-flop, a green bottle (no message, though he checked just in case), and a length of orange string. Then a hinged frame, a clothes-airer like the one Mum stood in the bath at home. When he pulled it open and stood it upright, pushing its legs into the stones, he thought of displaying various other items on it, like a weird selection of laundry, so he used the string to fasten the flip-flop to its rails. The bottle he tucked into the pebbles underneath. Then he walked along the line of sea-weed to see what else he could find.

A ragged sweatshirt was next, badly unravelled. When he turned back with that, he saw with indignation that the skinny boy – the one who'd been watching him yesterday – was standing by the clothes-airer, fiddling with it. Hal jogged back, ready for a confrontation.

'Hey, leave that alone!' he yelled, from a few metres away.

The boy looked at him, startled. He had a thin, pointy face and big eyes, and wore the same red hoodie and black knitted hat he'd had on before. Shrugging, he backed off at once.

'I only help,' he said. Hal saw that he'd been adding a contribution – he'd got a red plastic wheel, and was trying

74

to tie it to the bottom rung. He hadn't done it yet, because the string was too long and too tangly, and too strong to be snapped by hand; the wheel fell to the ground, and he made to move forward for it, but then looked anxiously at Hal. He was clearly afraid of being hit or grabbed. And now, up close, seeing how skinny and small the kid was, Hal gave up any idea of toughing it out. He'd been in trouble at school recently for picking on someone smaller than him (*picking* on! On Jason Green, stocky, shaven-headed, fiercer than ten Rottweilers!) and he knew at once that there was no point taking on this boy. It wouldn't even be a challenge.

'You can help if you want,' he conceded. This kid looked as lonely as he was. Why wasn't he at school? Had he been chucked out, too?

'Thank you!' The boy gave a big, shy smile. He spoke with some kind of accent. Maybe he was just here on holiday. Perhaps he didn't even speak much English.

Hal set off in one direction, the boy in the other. Soon he held up something and waved it at Hal – a Wellington boot. Hal didn't find anything new for a while apart from the broken skeleton of what must have once been a gull, with a few tattered feathers still attached. But by the time he went back to the clothes-airer with only a bedraggled striped sock to add, the foreign boy had amassed quite a collection: besides the boot, he'd found a DVD case, a sodden tennis ball, another bottle and a dog-bowl. He tied the boot to one side of the airer, while Hal arranged the other things underneath. But now the tide was lapping at their feet, sucking at the pebbles. Their strange work of art would soon be taken back by the sea. It was daft anyway – pointless.

'I go now,' said the boy. He hesitated. 'I watch you yesterday. When you make a big sand fish.'

'Uh.' Hal was trying to disentangle himself from the string. 'Yeah. Saw you too.'

'I come here again tomorrow. Hal, is your name? I heard the man call.'

Hal nodded. 'You?'

Again the wide, shy smile. 'I am Czeszka.'

'Say again? Chesska?'

'Czeszka. Franczeszka. Is Polish. Franczeszka Kazimierz.'

'*Uh*?' went Hal, and then, as if one image had been snatched away to be replaced by another, saw what he hadn't seen before – that the face smiling at him wasn't a boy's, but a girl's. She walked off fast, but turned to give him a friendly wave. He felt aggrieved, as if she'd deliberately set out to trick him.

'I've been sleeping and resting all day,' said Mum, on the phone. 'And being waited on hand and foot. I'll make the most of it, while it lasts!'

There she was, Mum, talking to him in her normal voice. Everything would be all right.

They chatted for a few minutes more; then Aunt Jude took over. 'Oh yes – yes, he's settled in fine, no trouble at all,' she told Mum. He expected her to add, 'Apart from scarpering down to the beach when I told him to stay in,' but she didn't.

When she'd finished, she passed the phone back to Hal for a final few words. 'Bye then, Prince Hal,' Mum said.

'Aunt Jude's going to bring you up to visit on Friday or Saturday, so I'll see you soon – but we'll talk again tomorrow.'

Hal went out into the garden feeling almost happy. Till his mobile made its plunking sound in his pocket. Message from Luke: U MIST GR8 MATCH WE WON 3-1 GREENY GOT HAT TRICK C YA.

Gaaah! The luck of Jason Green, cocky little— Three goals! There'd be no stopping him now. Hal chucked his mobile right across the lawn, then had to go and retrieve it from among thorny rose-stems, spiking his hands. He didn't bother answering. Typical Luke, that was, texting only to wind him up.

Don was back earlier today and had started making curry: he was grinding spices, chopping up onions and garlic. 'Not too much garlic, if you don't mind!' said Aunt Jude, kitchen assistant. 'I don't want to breathe fumes over everyone.' She was going out after they'd eaten, to her Tuesday choir practice.

Don's curry was delicious, better than any curry Hal had ever tasted in his life – the spicy flavours bursting in his mouth and on his tongue, the meat succulent. Aunt Jude hurried off to the Town Hall, and Hal helped Don with the clearing up. Then, because the evening was so mild and still, they went to the beach. It felt different there on the shore as darkness fell and the town lights came on; as if the sea was whispering secrets for just the two of them to hear. The tide was far out, obeying the pull of the moon; and there *was* the moon, a sliver of it, throwing a glimmery path out to sea.

'Clocks go back this weekend,' Don said. 'Then it'll really feel like winter's coming.'

They walked all the way along the sands, climbing over the limpet-clad groynes, as far as the old lifeboat-house, a flint-clad building with a big concrete ramp sloping down to the beach. Hal went over for a closer look, though Don was reluctant. 'I liked it the way it was,' he grumbled. 'Don't know why they have to go – k! – messing about with it.'

They wandered round to the landward side, where the changes were more obvious. There was a gravelled car park, with an electrician's van parked alongside and two cars. In a big glass extension to the old building, three men were at work: one high on a ladder, the others working at floor level. Hal saw a shiny wooden floor, and zig-zag screens standing ready. This must be the new gallery, where Amanda Whatsit wanted to put Don's paintings. That'd be cool, Hal thought; but all Don said, after one brief glance, was, 'They'll have to work round the clock to get that finished in time.'

It was gone ten when Aunt Jude came home. By then, Don had fallen asleep in front of the TV news, and Hal had zapped to a different channel.

'Come on, Hal, you should be in bed by now.' Aunt Jude sounded a bit flustered. Don was still snoring gently. She went over and shook him awake.

Hal thought she'd chivvy Don straight out of the house, round to the flat, but when Hal came out of the bathroom he could hear them talking. They were in the kitchen, Aunt Jude's voice low, Don's still a bit sleepy.

Afterwards, mentally replaying what he heard, over and over and over, Hal wasn't sure whether he'd paused deliberately to listen, or whether Aunt Jude's words had floated up to him.

'. . . What if Hal finds out?'

He heard that quite clearly, even though Aunt Jude seemed to be speaking in a quiet, urgent tone.

Finds out what?

A chill shivered through him as he stood. It had to be something about Mum, didn't it? Something bad, something terrible? What if she'd *died,* died suddenly in hospital, and Aunt Jude wasn't telling him?

Willing the floorboards not to creak, he crept down the stairs on bare feet. The kitchen door was ajar, and through the gap he saw Aunt Jude moving towards the table, and sitting down; Don was out of view. Hal crouched at the turn of the stairs, ears straining so hard that they seemed to be stretched out like antennae.

'—turn up now, of all times, with Hal here!' Aunt Jude was saying.

'*Who*'s turned up?' Don's words were muffled in a yawn.

For all his concentrating, Hal couldn't pick out the next bit; Aunt Jude had dropped her voice. He edged along towards the kitchen, alert, ready to dart back if anyone came out; his right ear was as close to the door-edge as he could get it without being seen.

'—nice young woman called Valerie. Her first time tonight,' said Aunt Jude.

Not bad news about Mum, then. But still – he had to know what this was about.

'So I chatted to her in the break,' Aunt Jude went on.

'She's new to Ryton, just moved here. But she told me her husband lived here till he was twenty-one, then spent some time in Jamaica, where they met. He's got family there.'

'Uh-huh,' went Don, as if he didn't see the point of all this.

'I didn't make the connection – why would I? – but when we finished he was waiting for her outside, in the car with two little girls asleep in the back. And she was keen to introduce me. Wesley! Wesley Prince! I nearly fell over. Tina's old boyfriend!'

'What, you mean he's . . .'

Hal couldn't hear the rest of what Don said, but then Aunt Jude spoke again:

'I'd never seen Hal till the funeral, remember. No, Tina's never said, and I've never asked – it's up to her whether she tells me or not. But as soon as I saw Hal, I knew it must be Wesley. *Has* to be.'

The words got inside Hal's head and zipped about like mosquitoes, dizzying him. They almost stopped him from hearing any more. He pressed forward. Concentrate. Keep still. Don't miss a word.

This Wesley she was talking about – his father – his *father*! He had to be – that was what Don had asked, wasn't it? Aunt Jude had just said so – she'd seen him – *spoken* to him! Did they all know, did everyone know? The blood throbbed in Hal's head, in his ears, even in his eyes. He'd managed to stand on his own foot, almost tripping; he extricated himself, and froze as the door creaked slightly, but no one noticed.

'He and Tina were practically joined at the hip,' said Aunt Jude, 'that last summer before I went off to Portugal. So now what? Now Wesley's here with his wife and family? Does he even know about Hal? Does *she* – Valerie, I mean? And should I tell Tina? Or not?'

'Can't you find out from this Wesley?'

'I couldn't do that! Go poking my nose in!'

Don humphed. 'Doesn't usually stop you.'

'But what if Wesley *doesn't* know?'

A pause, then: 'Well, he *ought* to, didn't he? If he's got a strapping young son? It's not fair to keep that from him.'

'Mmm,' went Aunt Jude. 'I suppose you're right. But that's Tina's business, not mine.'

She got up from the table and started clearing up. What they said now was drowned by the gush of water, clink of crockery, and cupboard doors closing, but then Hal heard distinctly, 'Anyway, I'd best be going,' from Don.

Hal darted, silent-footed, back to the stairs and up to the landing, where the banister rail hid him from view. Aunt Jude and Don came to the front door.

'See you tomorrow then. There's nothing you can do, so don't lose sleep over it,' Don said.

'OK,' Aunt Jude replied, in a *Yeah, right* kind of way; but then she said, 'Thanks, Don,' in a kinder voice. They hugged each other briefly, rather to Hal's surprise, then the front door opened and closed, and Don was gone. Aunt Jude slipped the chain across and stood there for a moment, deep in thought.

Hal couldn't think why Don didn't have a bed here, as he was around so much; but now his brain was on fast-spin, full of what he'd heard. He crept back to his room and sat on the bed.

Wesley Prince. Wesley Prince, who had been Mum's boyfriend. Who Aunt Jude said was his father. *Had* to be.

With family in Jamaica.

Prince Hal. That had always been Mum's nickname for him; he thought it was her way of saying he was special, her prince. And she'd told him about the Prince Hal in Shakespeare's play.

Prince Hal.

Was that because he might easily have been Hal Prince?

10
SEARCH

Two o'clock in the morning, and Hal was awake.

His brain was a knot of anger, confusion, excitement; his thoughts twined and tangled. He was too hot under his duvet, then he kicked it off and was cold. He was hungry, and thought of going down to the kitchen to find something to eat; next moment he thought he'd throw up. He was tired, utterly weary, but there was no way he could sleep.

The night seemed to be lasting for ever.

When Aunt Jude came upstairs after Don left, Hal had got into bed and pulled the duvet over himself, pretending to be asleep; he heard her come to his open door and pause there, then go to her own room. For a while he heard the burble of talk on her radio, until it was switched off and the house was in silence. Hal must have slept for a short while, but now he was fully awake, his new knowledge clear in his mind.

Wesley Prince.

His father. Mum's boyfriend.

Aunt Jude hadn't actually said he was black, but he *must* be, for her to think he was Hal's father. And he had family in Jamaica, and had met his wife there.

Only now did Hal remember the young woman he'd seen at the beach, with two little girls collecting shells. She'd smiled at him in a friendly, interested way. What were the names she'd called out? Grace, one of them – what was the other? He hadn't taken much notice at the time; just that they were black. And he hadn't registered the easy lilt of her accent, but heard it now as he replayed the scene in his head. Jamaican, it had to be, like Addis in year ten, who exaggerated the way he spoke because it sounded so cool.

How many Jamaican families could there be in Ryton-on-Sea, families with two young girls?

Wesley's wife. Wesley's wife – Valerie, wasn't that what Aunt Jude had said? And Wesley's little girls. They must be.

So those girls were his half-sisters? Weird that he hadn't known they existed till now, and they had no idea that *he* did.

The idea was like a bony finger jabbing at his ribs. He resented them for having a dad, when he didn't. They had *his* dad.

But—

Why couldn't Wesley and Mum have stayed together, if they were so keen on each other, like Aunt Jude said? Now it was all messed up. Mum with no boyfriend, Wesley with a wife and child. A Jamaican wife. Was that the problem with Mum? That she was white?

Was *Wesley* racist? That was one of the things Luke had come out with. That Hal wasn't black enough for his father to want him.

Not black enough, not good enough.

Hey, thanks, Luke. Thanks a lot. With friends like you—

Fidgeting, unable to settle, Hal rolled over and back again, the duvet twisting round his legs. He kicked himself free, sat up and turned on the light. He'd go raving mad before daylight, at this rate.

He could call Mum and demand that she told him what he already knew. 'I know about Wesley Prince,' he'd say. 'He's my father, isn't he?'

His mobile was in his hand; he got as far as selecting Mum's number, waiting for the ring tone. But what would she say back?

'Yes, Hal, but he doesn't know.'

'Yes, Hal, but he didn't want you. And he's got a family now.' (But did *Mum* know that?)

'No, Hal, he isn't. Whatever gave you that idea?'

Which would be worse? What would he do?

Anyway, she probably had her mobile turned off, in the hospital ward at night. He couldn't leave a message like that on Voicemail. He cancelled the call and sat turning his mobile over and over in his hands.

He had a father. At last. And his father was here in Ryton, quite close, not the vaguely distant Somewhere Else that had always been in his mind.

What'd he *do* about it?

Ask Mum. Tomorrow. He had to. Ask if it were true.

But would she tell him? She hadn't so far, had she? He'd asked and asked and *asked*, but never once had she said *Yes, you've got a father, and his name's Wesley Prince.*

So there must be some reason why she didn't want him to know.

Something bad about Wesley? Could that be it?

What he'd do, he decided, before he let on that he knew anything at all, was find Wesley Prince for himself. Get a look at him. His wife was in Aunt Jude's choir; she'd been down on the beach with the little girls. They'd be around. How hard could it be?

Turning on the bedside lamp, he opened the drawer of the small cabinet. There they were, like a kind of promise: the marbles his father – Wesley! – had given Mum. He reached in without looking and lifted out the first one his fingers closed round.

It was his favourite, the tiger's eye, with its glowing amber colour and its darker centre. It was a wise and knowing eye that gazed at him steadily. *I know,* it said. *I've always known.*

'Come on, sleepyhead! Time to get up.' Aunt Jude was bending over him, shaking him awake.

He blinked, and roused himself. 'Uh.' It was full daylight; the night had passed somehow, the darkness teeming with questions and questions and no real answers he could grab hold of.

'Goodness, you were fast asleep! Don must have tired you out. Come on down. Breakfast's ready and I need to leave in half an hour.'

She had another meeting today, she told Hal while he ate his cereal, about the sale of Marborough's. 'It's more complicated than I ever imagined. We've got an offer, but there's still lots to do. Solicitors, surveyors, planners, land registry – soon as I solve one problem, another one looms.'

Hal hardly knew how to look at her. At any moment the question might burst out of his mouth: *Why aren't you telling me you met Wesley Prince?*

Wesley Prince. His dad. His *dad*! A real person, a real live person who was living and breathing and moving about, not far from here. And he had a name, at last! Just the right name. Hal liked saying it to himself, silently. Hearing it, tasting it. Wesley. Prince. Wesleyprince.

Aunt Jude cleared away the dishes. 'Now, Hal, I'll be tied up most of the morning. But I'm trusting you to stay here and get on with your work. Then you can go out this afternoon. That worked well yesterday, didn't it?'

Hal nodded. Yesterday – it seemed light years away. He hadn't known, then.

Don arrived just as Aunt Jude was checking the files in her briefcase and taking her car keys from the hook; he feigned brief interest in Hal's history books and then left, saying he'd see Hal later.

Today, although he found it impossible to get his head round Divided Ireland, Hal did stay indoors. He had urgent things to do this afternoon, and it wasn't worth getting himself grounded. Whatever Aunt Jude said about trusting him, he knew she'd be checking up.

He sent a text to Osman, EMAIL L8R, and a curt single word to Luke. He doodled in his rough book. He wrote the name WESLEY in capitals and looked and looked at it until the letters jumbled themselves into nonsense.

At last he was free. As soon as he'd had a snack lunch with Aunt Jude, he pulled on his coat and was outside, jogging down the road, eager. He wanted the sea, the waves, the salt-laden wind on his face, but more urgent was his quest for Wesley Prince.

Wesley must have a job somewhere – or, if he didn't, he'd be looking for one. Wesley's wife would have to go shopping sometimes, take the little girls out, to a play-ground perhaps, or the beach again, or a nursery. Hal headed for the town centre.

Disappointingly, it was much like any other town – the street lined with estate agents, shoe shops, charity shops, a Co-op and a Tesco. He went into both supermarkets, along every aisle. He ventured inside both pubs, the Anchor and the Boatman, but a boy on his own attracted glances, and he quickly retreated to the street.

The shops along the sea-front had an end-of-season, closing-down look. Two cafés were open; Hal checked them out, looking in through the windows, but one was empty, and in the other an elderly man sat with a mug of tea, slipping bits of cake to his dog under the table. The amusement arcade was full of flickering and darting lights, but had only one bored-looking customer, a biker in leathers. The fish-and-chip shop wouldn't open till five, and most of the guesthouses had VACANCIES signs in their front windows, but in a rather hopeless way.

On the corner, where the promenade curved round and became the High Street, Marborough's stood big and empty, adding to the feeling of desertion. UNDER OFFER notices had now been stuck over the FOR SALE ones, so things must be moving along. Hal wished he'd been around when the store had been open. It would have been cool to wander round a big shop that had the same name as him. Maybe he could have got sports gear or something at a big reduction; but no, his grandfather would have been too mean for that.

Dispirited, Hal trailed back the way he'd come. This wasn't as easy as he'd hoped; he could search the town all day long, and still not find Wesley or his wife.

He went down to the beach and walked along towards the huts. The sea was a deep, still blue today, with big clouds heaped, dazzling white, so clearly defined that he could almost imagine himself climbing into them. The tide was halfway in, the good sand still exposed. He felt in his pocket for the two marbles he'd chosen this morning. There was no sign at all of the washing-airer construction he'd made with the foreign boy-now-girl – the tide had taken it. But when he looked, he found a plastic container that would be better than nothing to dig with. What he ought to do was raid his grandfather's garden shed for a proper trowel or spade.

He began to scoop and throw sand, to pat and mould and shape.

Not a whale this time, but the sandman of his dreams. Life-size; a big, tall man; arms by his sides, feet turned out. Having to beat the tide, Hal panted in his efforts, examining the figure from all sides, smoothing and improving.

He was so engrossed that he didn't see the girl, Czeszka, until she was a few metres away.

'Is good,' she said; no Hi or Hello.

Hal shrugged. He hadn't finished yet. He wished he could do more with the face, but at least he could provide eyes; he took out the two marbles and carefully placed them in position.

Czeszka laughed; she clapped her hands. 'Now he can see! Now he see us.'

Hal said nothing. He didn't want to share the sandman with anyone. He pinched sand into a better-shaped nose, then eyebrows, and lips. His silence didn't deter Czeszka; she fetched a handful of pebbles and a strand of glossy seaweed, dark red. Laughing delightedly, she gave the man a row of buttons as if for a jacket, and a seaweed scarf. Although he didn't really want to, Hal joined in, finding a different kind of seaweed that resembled hair.

'Now he's just a raggy old scarecrow,' he told Czeszka.

Arranging more of the fringey stuff to make a beard, she frowned, puzzled. 'Please? Scarecrow?'

'In fields. Like this.' He mimed stick arms and a glum face.

He couldn't tell if Czeszka understood, but she seemed to find it hilarious. She had a go too, and said something in Polish, and gestured that she wanted him to say it back. He wasn't sure about this: not keen on hanging out with a girl. What if someone *saw*?

It was all spoiled now, anyway. The sandman had turned into a joke, with his buttons and beard, not the real, solemn man-figure of Hal's dream. Anger rose in him like a tide.

The first waves were lapping at the sand feet, but Hal was too impatient to wait. He snatched up the marble eyes, dropping them into his pocket. Then he jumped into the middle of the sandman's chest, landing hard. He stamped, kicked up sand in a wave, trampled and pounded in a furious dance, until the man-figure was reduced to a muddle of footmarks and half-buried trails of seaweed.

Czeszka watched in dismay, standing back. And now the water was washing around Hal's feet, sloshing into his trainers. He began to feel ridiculous, the way she stood watching. He turned it into a joke, stamping up water, dashing out of the way just in time as the next big wave washed up the beach. Only a few smooth bumps showed where the sandman had been, as the wave sucked back. Czeszka made a sorrowful sound; but what did she expect? There was no way they could hold back the tide.

Seeming relieved that his burst of temper was over, she joined in, dashing into the shallows, leaping back just in time to avoid a soaking. Then she set off at a fast run, looking round as if she wanted Hal to follow.

He didn't. He stood panting at the edge of the pebbles. His jeans were drenched, and felt cold and clammy. There was no way she'd get him splashing about like a little kid.

Czeszka turned, and came back close enough to call out. 'I go now!' She looked at him keenly. 'Tomorrow?'

Hal shrugged. 'Maybe. Maybe not.'

She hesitated, then set off again, jogging along the tide's edge, her trainers sending up spray. He wondered where she lived, and why she wasn't in school.

Was it worth trying the town again? He was caught between the urge to try, and the disappointment of another failure. Looking along the row of beach huts, he saw Don walking across the shingle. Apart from flip-flop sandals, he wore nothing but a pair of khaki shorts. His body was skinny, very brown where the sun had reached – shins, arms and hands, face – and alarmingly white everywhere else. He was a two-tone man.

Seeing Hal, he waved. He kicked off the flip-flops just above the tide mark, and continued picking his way, awkward now, wincing over the stones. As soon as he reached the sand, he began to run: into the waves, throwing up spray, slowing as he reached deeper water.

Stop! Hal wanted to shout, with the crazy idea that Don was going to swim out and out, and never come back.

As soon as he was in deep enough, Don launched himself into a powerful crawl. He did head out, but then he paused, looked back at Hal and turned to swim parallel to the shore.

Hal was impressed. Tomorrow he might swim too. He hadn't thought of bringing his Speedos; still, he'd be a wuss not to go in. It'd be cold, he knew that from the damp clamminess around his legs, but if Don could do it then so could he.

Now he'd wasted the whole afternoon, wandering round town and mucking about with Czeszka, and he hadn't found out a single thing more about Wesley Prince. Still, there was this evening. He'd see what he could get from Aunt Jude.

11
HIMSELF

His chance came after supper, when Don said he was going back to the beach hut to carry on painting. Aunt Jude had put the kettle on for coffee, but now said she might as well wait till Don came in, later.

Hal had planned this: an indirect approach seemed best.

'Mum said you used to stick up for her when there was trouble.' He made his voice as casual as he could. 'What, school trouble?'

Aunt Jude sat down again, sideways in her chair. 'Only when she got into the sixth form. She'd always done well at school. Then Gerry – your grandad – didn't like some of the people she started going round with, out of school as well as in.'

This sounded promising. 'What people?'

'There was a girl called Miranda, I remember. Suddenly she was your mum's best friend. Gerry said she was leading Tina astray – always having mad ideas, like hitch-hiking to Morocco, giving up school to pick grapes in France, buying a clapped-out van and setting off across Europe. Gap year,

93

people call it now. This Miranda treated every year as a gap year.'

'Mum's got a friend called Miranda,' Hal said. 'She lives in Scotland.'

Aunt Jude nodded. 'Might be the same one. I don't know. Then there were parties, boys, wanting to stay out all night on the beach, with a camp-fire. Your grandad was a bit strict and old-fashioned, I suppose – wanted Tina to stay at home, be tucked up in bed by eleven o'clock even on Saturday nights. He thought she was throwing away her chances at school.'

'*Was* she?'

'Well, I don't know.' Aunt Jude dabbed at some spilled grains of salt. 'People need to have fun. She's a clever girl. She'd have done what she wanted in the end.'

So, did she, Hal wondered? He asked, 'What *did* she want?'

'At first she wanted to be a marine biologist. Then it was psychology. That's what she went to university for.'

'She left, though, didn't she?' Hal asked. 'What changed her mind?'

'I don't know,' Aunt Jude said, quite abruptly. 'Besides, that was about the time I went to work in Portugal. Then in the south of France. That's where I met Don. So I didn't have much to do with your mum and grandparents for quite a few years – just kept in touch through postcards and odd phone calls.'

Hal needed to steer the conversation back to Wesley. 'Boys, you said? Didn't her dad want her to have a boy-friend?'

'Oh, no boy was ever going to be good enough for Tina as far as Gerry was concerned,' Aunt Jude said, smiling.

'So – when they, you know, had the big bust-up, when they stopped talking to each other, was that cos Mum had a boyfriend he didn't like?'

Aunt Jude's glance slithered away from Hal's; he had the feeling of reaching a roadblock. 'I don't know.'

'But you *do* know,' Hal burst out. 'You do!'

'Hal, I'm sorry but I really don't. I told you, I wasn't here.'

Hal shoved his chair back and got up from the table, clumsily, so that the corner jabbed into his thigh.

You're lying. He almost said it, but she put out a hand to restrain him.

'Hal – I know you've got questions. Big, important questions. But you'll have to ask your mum. She's the only one who can tell you what you want to know.'

What, she thought he never *had*?

'Ask your mum,' Aunt Jude repeated. 'Only not this week, eh? Let her get out of hospital first.'

Aunt Jude stayed home next day, busy with phone calls and emails. The morning dragged by. Hal tried to read two more chapters of his English book, but his eyes kept gliding over the same paragraph without taking in its meaning. For art, he was supposed to do some sketching, but there was no point doing that here when he could go down to Don's and the beach later. He was hopeless at drawing, anyway. Modelling, making things – that was better.

What about getting *Don* to draw something for him,

and handing that in – see if Mr Smithson recognised a genuine Don Inchbold when he held one in his hands, something by a real famous artist, that people would pay money for?

'What are you grinning at?' asked Aunt Jude, across the table.

'Uh. Nothing.'

'You look a bit more cheerful, anyway.'

Yeah, right. Only because the pox-faced clock had tocked away most of the morning and he'd soon be let out.

The instant he was free, he was out of the door and running. Running hard, his feet slapping the pavement, arms pumping – as if sheer speed would find Wesley, run him to ground like a hunted animal. When he reached Marborough's, though, Hal slowed and stopped, panting. Where? Where to try now?

There were parts of Ryton he hadn't explored yet. He needed a plan; no use just wandering about. He skirted round the High Street this time, and turned into the A-road with the sign pointing to the station and the leisure centre. This brought him close to the primary school Mum had pointed out, the school she'd gone to as a girl.

He reached the railings and stopped. Lights were on inside, and he could see bright wall displays. He heard the sound of tambourines and a piano, and the loud encouraging voice of a teacher from one of the classrooms; in a glass-fronted hall he saw gym apparatus and very small children sitting in a semi-circle on the floor. So there were infant classes as well as junior. Maybe Wesley's two daughters came here?

He couldn't clearly remember the two little girls, not having looked at them very closely. They could be too young for school. But, if one of them *did* come here, wouldn't Wesley's wife have to come and collect her at the end of the day?

Maybe he'd hang around. Or come back in an hour or so: he looked at his watch. Coming up to two. What time would school finish – three, half-past? It was worth checking out – a place where mothers would gather and stand chatting.

He turned away, wondering where to go meanwhile – then *saw* her, walking along on the other side of the street. His heart thumped loudly in his chest. The very person he'd been looking for! It was, wasn't it? The young mother he'd seen down on the beach. She wore track pants and white trainers and a loose coat, and was pushing a buggy with the smaller of the two girls in it. The little girl was singing to herself, the mother smiling, and prompting her with words. She didn't notice Hal watching. And she didn't cross the road to the school; instead she pushed on briskly, over the zebra crossing at the corner, and down a side street.

When Hal was quite sure she hadn't noticed him, he followed, a good distance behind. She was heading for the leisure centre – a large new building of steel and glass at the inland edge of town, with playing fields behind it and the rise of the Downs beyond. A car park, half full, occupied the space in front. On the floor above, Hal saw people pumping away at fitness machines and exercise bikes. The entrance doors stood wide open.

In she went, Wesley's wife – if that's who she was – while Hal hesitated outside. What now? He'd hoped she was heading home, so that he could find out where Wesley lived. Instead she must be going to an exercise class or to work out on her own in the gym.

Might as well go in, now he was here. He could pick up a leaflet, see if there was football coaching or anything else he might want to do.

Inside, the foyer was enormous. He was facing a reception area, where two staff stood behind a counter: a black man, and a younger blonde woman. The woman with the buggy had pushed it right up to the counter, and now the man had come out from behind, to scoop up the little girl in his arms. 'Give Daddy a kiss,' he said, in a laughing voice.

Daddy! Was this *him,* actually him?

Hal's eyes blurred, staring. Or had he got it wrong – made it all up, when this family had nothing to do with him?

He felt as conspicuous as if caught in spotlights, but no one was looking his way. He stepped back a few paces and pretended to be examining a noticeboard; he felt hot and awkward, in danger of falling over his feet. The little girl chuckled delightedly, then the man put her down and said, 'See you later, sweetheart. You be good, now,' and waved as she and her mother moved off towards a door labelled CRÈCHE, with ducks and rabbits painted on it.

The man went back to his position, and Hal heard the blonde woman say, 'She's so gorgeous,' and the man's smiling reply, 'Oh, yeah, cute as a kitten.' Then he noticed Hal, and called, 'You OK, there? Need any help?'

Hal tried to look normal as he walked over. He looked at the man's handsome, friendly face.

'I'm – uh – I'm—' Hal blathered.

'Yes?' said the man, waiting to be helpful.

'Is there a – like – a form to fill in?' Hal said in a rush.

'Sure.' The man handed him one from a pile. 'You thinking of joining? You live in town?'

'Jus' thinking 'bout it.' Something was stopping Hal's words from getting out normally, but the man nodded and said, 'You have a read of this. Get your mum or dad to sign the form if you'd like to join. Or you can just pay per session if that's easier. And – look—' He gave Hal a separate sheet. 'There's special half-term activities all next week. You don't need to be a member for those. Have a look, see if you'd like to come.'

'Uh, thanks.' And now Hal's eyes swung to the sign on the wall behind – a slotted bracket into which a card had been placed saying DUTY MANAGER: WESLEY PRINCE. This *was* him. *Him*! Really *him*! Hal could hardly stand upright, hardly breathe normally. And just in case there could be any doubt, the man wore a badge saying WESLEY PRINCE, CENTRE MANAGER, with the running-man logo.

Hal was face to face with – actually talking to—

He stared and stared, taking in as much as he could of Wesley Prince. The glossy dark skin, the very white teeth, the brown eyes that looked at him kindly. He was tall, over six feet, Hal guessed. Fit and athletic – well, he ought to be, working in a sports centre. Smart, in the blue sweat top that must be the centre uniform, as the woman wore the same. The sleeves were pushed up, showing muscular forearms.

'OK, then?' Wesley Prince was saying. 'Have a look round now, if you like? I can get someone to show you around.'

'No. No. Thanks.' Was he imagining it, or had the

kindly gaze turned suspicious? Hal looked around in confusion. There were chairs and low tables; through glass doors he saw a café. 'I'll just – er – get a drink—' he mumbled.

'Fine! Take your time. No pressure,' said Wesley.

Moving towards the drinks machine, Hal chose a seat that gave a good view of the desk. Wesley Prince picked up some papers and went through to an office behind, leaving the blonde woman in charge of reception. While Hal waited to see if he'd come back, Wesley's wife returned from the crèche; another woman coming through the main doors called 'Hi, Valerie,' and they went upstairs together, talking and laughing.

Hal felt dizzy, his mind buzzing, sparking with impressions. With hope and doubt. With a hundred new questions.

Wesley Prince. He'd met Wesley Prince. Spoken to him.

And – Wesley Prince was exactly the kind of father he'd hoped for. Fit, tall, handsome. Friendly and approachable. A father to be proud of. Hal imagined himself walking in the street with Wesley, meeting people: Wesley would say, 'This is my son, Hal.' He'd say it like that, to show that Hal was the son he'd always wanted.

But did Wesley *know*?

Hal could tell him, now. Go to the desk and ask to speak to him. Wesley would come to the counter, ready to listen to whatever request Hal had. And Hal would say, 'My name's Hal. Hal Marborough,' to see what effect that had.

But what next? Would Wesley's face show recognition? Shock? Guilt? What would he say – what *could* he say? Marborough, Mum's name, he'd know that – but did he know Hal existed? And if he hadn't known, what then?

In a turmoil of indecision, Hal got to his feet and walked over to the desk. The blonde receptionist gave him a bright, expectant look; behind her, in the office, Hal saw Wesley Prince seated in front of a computer screen, with papers spread out next to the keyboard.

'Yes – how can I help you?' the woman prompted.

'I—' Hal began; then changed his mind, and mumbled vaguely about coming back later. He veered away and out of the wide doors to the car park. She must think he was a total space cadet. On the plus side, he knew now where Wesley worked, where Wesley could be found again. When he wasn't at work, the staff would know when his next shift was.

Centre Manager. A good job. The kind of job Hal would have wanted his father to have. Wesley was a dad to stand up next to Luke's; Luke's dad was sporty and fit but had a boring job in insurance.

Hal felt so energised, his whole body fizzing with it, that he ran all the way to the beach. He was making for Don's, but as he reached the first of the beach huts he stopped, seeing huge letters drawn in the sand.

HAL
CZESZKA HERE
BY

A peeled stick lay nearby, discarded, but Czeszka was nowhere in sight. Hal puzzled over the message. So that was how she spelled her name – he'd thought it was Chesska. But what did it mean? Czeszka *was* here? Or Czeszka *will* be here? He hadn't said anything about meeting her, had he? She had no reason to expect anything from him. Still, he picked up the stick and wrote 2MORO below her words. She probably wouldn't see it before the tide washed in.

Don was sitting in the doorway of his hut staring out at the sea, doing nothing at all.

'Aren't you painting today?' Hal asked him.

'Can't paint all day long. Have to sit and think.'

Now that he was here, Hal felt an urge to tell Don all about his discovery. *I've found him. My dad. My DAD. Seen him. Talked to him. I know where he works.*

But no, of course he couldn't. Not without making Don promise, first, not to tell Aunt Jude. Once Wesley knew, then things would be different. Already Hal was imagining himself in a Luke-type arrangement, living with Mum but spending alternate weekends with his dad – with Wesley. It was just a shame that Wesley was married already, so there was no chance of him getting together with Mum.

'Hey, relax!' Don told him. 'You're making me anxious, jittering about like that. What's up – ants in your pants?'

'Oh. Nothing.' Hal sat on the step, but couldn't be still; with a piece of broken shell he poked and raked at the grains of dry sand that had blown and collected in the angle of the doorstep.

'You missed your girlfriend, if that's what's biting you.' Don gave him an amused look. 'She was here about an hour ago. Said she'd be at the lifeboat-house.'

'She's not my girlfriend,' Hal mumbled, indignant. 'I don't even know her.'

Don shrugged. 'Up to you.' He got stiffly to his feet. 'It *is* about time I did some work, though. Hang around if you want. Or maybe you need to burn off some of that energy.'

Hal looked at his watch; he had an hour before Aunt Jude would expect him back at the house. He might as well go and see what Czeszka was up to. 'OK. See you later,' he told Don, and set off along the beach, breaking into a run, his trainers biting into the pebbly sand.

He could have run for miles and miles. Weird, how different he felt. Taller. More confident. More excitingly himself.

12
FAMILY

Having expected Czeszka to be sitting on the ramp on the lifeboat-house, flicking stones perhaps, waiting for him, he was surprised to find her inside, in the new extension. Work was still going on there: two electricians were positioning spotlights in the roof-joists, and a young man in overalls was tidying up. Czeszka was helping him, carrying stuff out to a white van parked on the gravel.

Hal loitered by the entrance until she saw him. At once she came over, carrying a bucket.

'What you doing?' he asked, looking at the bucket.

'I help my brother. Gregor. He work here three days.' Czeszka called to the young man, rapidly and incomprehensibly. He came over too, held out his hand for a formal handshake and said, 'Please to meet you.' He had a very deep voice and a quick, alert expression, like his sister's.

'You live in Ryton?' Hal asked Czeszka, while Gregor climbed inside the van to stow things properly. 'I mean you're not just here on holiday?'

'Yes, my family all here. Gregor is plasterer.' She managed to put a *z* in it. 'Our father is chef at Ocean Hotel since one year. Now my mother and I come also to live, and Gregor to study. I start at Southdean School after the half-time holiday.'

Hal grinned. 'Half-*term*.'

'Thank you. Half-term,' Czeszka repeated. 'Yes, I wish you tell me when wrong.'

'What year you in?'

'Year?'

'Yeah, year. You know. At school.'

'Oh. I see.' She thought for a moment. 'Year nine I think is called.'

So she was the same age as him. When he'd thought she was a boy, she'd looked younger, but now it was hard to tell.

Gregor climbed into the driver's seat, and spoke to Czeszka in Polish, adding, 'Bye,' to Hal before driving off.

'He did this. Good work, yes?' Czeszka swept an arm towards the high wall that backed onto the original lifeboat-house, and was now smoothly and flawlessly skimmed in plaster. 'And you?' she added. 'Family?'

Hal hesitated, then said, 'Yes. My dad lives here. He works at the sports centre.'

It was good, how that sounded. And true.

That evening, while they ate supper, Hal saw Don watching him closely. Don knew he'd been agitated earlier, but Hal wasn't going to let Aunt Jude know why. If Don thought Czeszka was the big secret, that might be a good thing. Hal hid his excitement behind a front of bored gruffness, barely looking up from his plate, hardly speaking except to answer questions with monosyllabic grunts.

He managed to speak to Mum on the phone without giving anything away. Then, when he'd positioned himself at the dining table with Aunt Jude's laptop and was about to email Osman, the phone rang again. He didn't take a lot of notice; heard Aunt Jude reassuring whoever it was that Yes, everything was fine; then she said, 'All right, I'll fetch him,' and appeared in the doorway.

'It's your grandad,' she told him. 'From Spain. He wants a word with you.'

'With *me*? What about?'

'I expect he'll tell you.'

Slouching to his feet, Hal mumbled, 'Do I have to?' but Aunt Jude shushed him, a finger to her lips. She put the receiver firmly in his hand, and left him to it.

'Uh. Hello,' he said, in a toneless voice.

'Hal!' said the grandfather's voice. 'It's good to hear you. Your Aunt Jude is really enjoying having you around, you know. I hope you like being at the seaside?'

He sounded just like he had at the funeral: falsely cheery, as if speaking to a six-year-old.

' 'Sall right,' Hal replied.

'Sleeping in your mother's old bedroom, eh? That must feel a bit peculiar.'

Hal said nothing. Yes, it did when he thought about it, but all he could imagine now was Mum in her room dreaming about Wesley, and the grandfather spoiling it all.

There was a small cough at the end of the line, and the voice went on, 'Anyway, Hal, I'm looking forward to seeing you when I get back. It's grand out here but there's nowhere as good as home, is there? So I'll – er – see you soon. Goodbye, then – and keep your pecker up.'

'See you,' Hal said, and put the phone down.

Keep your pecker up! He was like someone in an ancient film. No one talked like that, no one in this century, anyway.

'OK?' said Aunt Jude, from the kitchen where she was cleaning the hob. He knew she'd been listening. Don was in the front room watching TV.

Hal shrugged. 'Is he coming back, then?'

She looked at him. 'Well, this *is* his house. He lives here.'

'Yeah, I know, but – like, soon?'

'Second week in November.' Aunt Jude looked at the kitchen calendar. 'That's right. His flight's booked for the seventh.'

Hal was relieved. 'I'll be home by then.' But at once he was caught in dismay: how could he go back home and carry on as before, when Wesley was *here*?

'He wants to make an effort,' Aunt Jude said. 'Make up for all the wasted years. I think your grandmother dying made him see things differently.'

Bit late for that, Hal thought. Thirteen years too late.

'And,' Aunt Jude went on, 'if he knows he's been stupid, done himself out of all the pleasure of having a daughter and a grandson, shouldn't he have a chance to put things right? Your mum wouldn't have come to the funeral, would she, or agreed to you coming here, if *she* didn't think so. I'd hate – you know I'd really hate for *him* to get old and die without things being sorted out.'

'S'pose.' Hal couldn't think of anything else to say. But,

really, he didn't see that it was up to him. He didn't see how both Wesley *and* the grandfather could fit into his life.

Later, in bed, he planned and planned ways of approaching Wesley, what to say. He'd forgotten, till Mum reminded him, that Aunt Jude was driving him up to the hospital tomorrow. He'd have no time to himself at all. He'd see Mum; but at the moment he felt awkward about that, too. Never before had he kept such a big secret from her.

Still, how could she blame him, when she'd kept her own secret for years and years?

Soon after lunch, Hal was in the passenger seat of Aunt Jude's silver Focus, setting off for the hospital.

How odd it felt, how dull, once they'd driven over the Downs to the flat land beyond. Not to feel the pull of the sea, not to see the shining water, the big sky, the heaped clouds. Away from the coast, every direction looked the same, flat and uninteresting: too many roads, too many directions, with no sense of the land's edge. Here, you'd have no idea whether the tide was in or out. Hal felt as if he must always have lived by the sea, he missed it so much.

In less than two hours, they were finding a parking space outside the huge modern hospital, and following signs for Wards, past Orthopaedics and Maternity, X-Ray and Theatre and Outpatients. A friendly male nurse directed them to Mum's bed, in a bay of four.

There she was: in her blue dressing-gown, sitting up in a chair beside her high bed. She looked pale and tired, but gave Hal a big hug. He smelled her familiar scent and the stuff she put on her hair, and felt as if they'd been separated for weeks and weeks.

She wasn't alone: Claire was there, arranging a big sheaf of lilies in a vase on the bedside cabinet. And there were three other women in the bay, one lying in bed, the other two sitting out, but none of them with any visitors. How could you tell anybody anything, so publicly, so exposed?

First there were introductions, as Claire and Aunt Jude hadn't met before. Then Mum wanted to know all about Hal's week and what he'd been up to, and how he liked Ryton. He gave evasive replies, saved by Aunt Jude's interruption: 'But what about *you*? How are you getting on?'

Mum told them about the little bits of progress she'd made each day, walking the length of the ward, being allowed to have a shower. 'They're probably letting me out tomorrow,' she told them, 'once the consultant's been round. But I've got to take things carefully for a while yet. No lifting, no getting tired. That's why I'll be staying at Claire's, for next week at least. She's offered to look after me.'

'Quite right too. It'll be fun,' said Claire. 'You'd only be bored at home, and – I know you! – you'll start cleaning windows, or sorting out cupboards.'

'And – Hal – Claire's got another suggestion,' Mum said, smiling at him.

'Yes. I thought you could come and stay too, Hal. I've got the space, with Stephen away – your mum'll have the guest room, and you can have his.'

'That'll be good, won't it?' said Mum. 'It's half-term – you'll be able to see your friends and go to your usual places. Aunt Jude can bring you up on Sunday.'

So they'd discussed it on the phone, Hal thought. No one had told *him.*

'No!' he burst out. 'I don't have to, do I? I want to stay where I am!'

'Hal!' Mum reproved. 'It's very kind of Claire – a lot of upheaval, whatever she says—'

'I just thought you'd rather be with your mum,' said Claire; but she sounded a bit relieved.

'Yeah, but not – I mean it's not like being at home. I like it at Aunt Jude's. The sea, and Don, and—' The thought of leaving Ryton made Hal feel panicky and sick. Even if he *didn't* go to Claire's, he'd only have another week there.

'It's fine with me, if Hal prefers to stay on,' Aunt Jude assured Mum. 'No problem at all. We like having him.'

'Oh well, if you're sure. But thanks again for offering, Claire. It's really kind of you – isn't it, Hal?'

'Yeah,' said Hal, able to produce a smile now that he definitely wasn't going. Imagine! Being snatched away from Ryton, so tantalisingly soon after making such a breakthrough!

There'd be no chance of talking to Mum on her own, however much he did or didn't want to tell her. A friendly black nurse arrived to check Mum's blood pressure; then a trolley came round with cups of tea. And now Mum was talking about a new worry.

'Jacky came to visit yesterday. And – well, it was a bit of a shock. She didn't want to tell me, but I could see she was holding something back, so I got it out of her. JJ's is closing down. I won't have a job to go back to.'

'What?' and 'Why?' from Claire and Aunt Jude.

'She hasn't been doing specially well lately – there are so many new hairdressers opening up all the time! – and now the rent's gone up, too,' Mum explained. 'She's decided to cut her losses. She was really apologetic about it, but she's made up her mind.'

Aunt Jude asked, 'What will you do?' and Claire made sympathetic noises. Hal said nothing, but looked at Mum in dismay. What – she'd be jobless? On the dole? What if she couldn't pay the rent? What if they lost the flat as well? What if—

Mum sighed. 'I don't know. I can't think about it, yet. I'll look around and see what I can find. It might turn out for the best. I never intended to be a hairdresser for my whole working life.'

They chatted a while longer, until it was time for the patients' supper. Claire left at that point; Hal and Aunt Jude waited while Mum picked at quiche and salad. Soon after, Aunt Jude said that she and Hal ought to be on their way. 'Friday traffic's always busy.'

'Thanks for coming.' Mum looked suddenly small and alone beside the high hospital bed, huddled into her dressing-gown.

'Don't worry too much about the job,' Aunt Jude told her in an undertone. 'Something'll turn up. It will, I promise.'

Hal wasn't sure how fragile Mum was, but she caught him in a big hug, and whispered, 'Bye, Prince Hal. I'll see you again soon as soon.'

Soon as soon was one of the things she used to say when he was little. And Prince Hal! She'd said it again! He almost said, 'I know why you call me that,' but the words jammed in his throat, and all he managed was a strangled, 'See you.'

He followed Aunt Jude back into the main aisle of the ward; he turned and saw Mum watching him, as if hanging on to the very last glimpse. Abruptly, embarrassingly, he felt as tearful as an infant. A big choking sob was building up in his chest; he could have cried, really cried, if he'd wanted to.

'What you said – about something turning up? How can you be so sure?' he asked Aunt Jude, to deflect attention. She wasn't planning to open up a hairdresser's just to give Mum a job, that was for sure.

'I don't know, yet,' said his great-aunt. 'But we'll think of something. We're family, and families help each other out.'

13

GLASS

Out in the garden, Aunt Jude was raking leaves and tidying. Hal, sure that she was safely occupied, was poring over the local telephone directory.

Priestman . . . Prill . . . Primrose . . . *Prince.*

There it was, springing out at him from the page.

Prince, W. 10 *The Strand, Ryton-on-Sea.* And the phone number.

Quickly he wrote it on a page torn from his rough book. He tucked the directory back into place on the shelf below the phone, and raced up to his room.

He'd rehearsed and rehearsed what to say, but still he hesitated. It would come out wrong, or his throat would clam up and he wouldn't be able to speak at all. But he made himself do it. With a trembling finger he keyed in the number, and waited.

The ringing tone went on for a long time; he realised he was holding his breath. He felt ready to howl with frustration and sag with relief, both at once. Then came the click of someone picking up.

'Yes?' said a man's voice – a cracked, out-of-breath voice, not Wesley's.

'Uh – I – is Wesley Prince there?' Hal asked, remembering to add, 'Please.'

'No, no, no. This is *Willard* Prince,' said the voice. 'You want my son Wesley. He's not here, he's in Marine Terrace. This is who?'

'Hal,' said Hal, greatly daring.

'OK then, Hal, here's his number. You ready?'

Hal wrote it down, thanked the man, and rang off. Then he paused, realising what he'd just done. One brief phone call had given him not only Wesley's phone number and address (though he'd forgotten to ask what number the house was) but also a *grandfather*. Not the miserable old man whose house this was, but a real, kindly-voiced grandfather. Jamaican, by his accent, the way his voice leaned into the words. Hal could almost picture him: stooped, with a lined face, and tightly curled hair gone iron grey with age. He'd have been sitting in his garden, or yard perhaps, reading the paper in the autumn sunshine. Or maybe he grew vegetables: Jamaican vegetables, red hot chilli peppers, in a greenhouse. Did he have a wife? If so, she'd be Hal's grandmother. A whole family was making itself at home in his imagination.

Here was his missing half! The half he'd always missed, wondered about. Jamaican. He was part-Jamaican. And Wesley had more family there: Aunt Jude had said so, to Don. Visions of beaches and carnivals, sounds of drumbeat and rap music filled Hal's mind. His. Part of him. He wanted to go there, see where he came from. See where that part of him belonged.

And now?

Instead of phoning, he'd go and find Wesley's house. That shouldn't be too difficult. Hal dipped his hand into the bag of marbles and probed with his fingers, choosing two by feel.

He'd pulled out two moon marbles, as he called them – the milky-white, swirly ones that seemed somehow mysterious. There were only two of those, so it seemed lucky to pick both. Could you make up your own super-stitions? Maybe he'd know by the end of today. For now, he'd believe it meant good luck. He slipped the marbles into his jeans pocket.

Aunt Jude had said that he didn't have to do school-work at the weekend, as long as all assignments were completed by Monday week. She was planning to take him out this afternoon, to Sea Life at Brighton, so he'd take his chance now.

'I'm getting lunch early,' she told him, when he said he was going out for a bit. 'So make sure you're back by twelve-thirty.'

No doubt she had a map of the town, but if he asked for it she'd want to know why. No prob – he'd ask some-one the way. But as he walked along near Marborough's he came across a town plan on a board, with YOU ARE HERE, and a red arrow pointing. An index at the bottom listed street-names: Marine Terrace was on the west side of town, one street up from the children's playground. Quite a short street, it looked on the plan, so he should be able to find out which house was Wesley's.

Five minutes later he was standing by a corner shop, with Marine Terrace stretching no more than two hundred metres in front of him. There were houses on one side of the street only, which made it easier; on the other, a steep bank with flowerbeds cut into it sloped down to the promenade, and the children's boating-pool. The houses were three-storey, most of them tall and narrow, without gardens in front.

The shop was the kind that sold newspapers, drinks and ice-creams as well as packets and cans of food. There were a few customers inside, and an approachable-looking woman stood behind the counter, so Hal went in. A man with a spaniel was buying a *Daily Express*, and talking about the weather forecast; when he'd finished, Hal bought a can of Sprite and asked the woman if she knew where Wesley Prince lived.

'Number fourteen, few doors along,' she told him. He saw how she looked at him, taking in the colour of his skin. Maybe she made the connection – guessed he was a relation.

The spaniel man had stopped in the doorway to roll up his newspaper and give it to the dog to carry in its mouth.

'Looking for Wesley, you say? You just missed him,' he told Hal. 'See him go along the road, I did, not five minutes ago, with his missus and the kids and the buggy.'

'Which way?'

'Down along the front, I 'spect.'

Uncertain now, Hal left the shop and turned in that direction. He'd tentatively planned what to say when he knocked at the house door, but now, instead, found himself in pursuit. He wanted Wesley on his own, not with his wife and children all listening. But at the very least he had to see where they'd go, and what they'd do.

There they were, walking along the promenade. Wesley was pushing the buggy with the smaller child in it; the older girl was skipping ahead. Valerie wore a green brimmed hat at a jaunty angle, and a bright green scarf.

Hal caught up a little, without getting so close that they'd see him following, then adjusted his pace to theirs. They were dawdling, pausing to look at boats far out to sea, and at a group of dark birds flying low over the shore, and then at the big noticeboard by the lifeboat-house. Here Hal hung well back, seeing Czeszka's brother Gregor standing outside talking to an older man. He didn't want Gregor to see him and wave.

Wesley's older daughter was impatient to move on. She was playing a stepping-and-counting game with herself, taking giant steps. 'Wait, Vera!' Valerie called to her, then joined in for a few moments, pretending it was harder than it was. Hal heard Wesley laughing as they walked on towards the park entrance. It was a boring kind of park, just paths and flowerbeds, trees and benches, and an ice-cream hut closed up for winter: Hal had briefly looked in there on his first day of searching.

But, instead of heading in through the gates, the Princes took a path that stayed close to the sea, dipping down below a line of trees that fringed the park. WORKSHOPS OPEN, Hal read, but before he'd seen any more, footsteps pounded behind him, and a voice called, 'Hal!'

He froze. Czeszka. Damn! She was running towards him, catching up fast. It was too late to pretend he hadn't seen her, and he couldn't tell her to go away.

Had Wesley heard? No – he was bending to adjust the fastening on Vera's shoe. Valerie had taken over pushing the buggy.

Czeszka reached him, breathing hard.

'I call, but you walk by. Where are you go? To see glass?'

'What?' Out of the corner of his eye, Hal saw Wesley and his family moving on towards a courtyard area, where a few people sat at café tables by the open double doors of a barn. There were square planters, a tree growing in each one, and window-boxes bright with flowers.

'Glass blow!' Czeszka was still panting. 'I watch last week with Gregor. Come, see.'

A sign by the barn door said GLASS-BLOWING DEMONSTRATIONS DAILY. Wesley's group had gone towards a sign marked POTTERY – HAND-THROWN CERAMICS, on the far side of the café. Beyond that, Hal saw STONEMASON'S WORKSHOP and SILVER MOON JEWELLERY. Reluctant to lose sight of Wesley, but unable to keep following without making it obvious, Hal gave way, and followed Czeszka into the dimly lit barn. His eyes adjusted. One end of the big space was occupied by display-cases filled with glasses and goblets, jewellery and ornaments, all spotlit to show the glancing colours. Farther in was a workshop area, where the demonstration was about to start.

It was fiercely hot at that end; Hal felt the heat striking him, sweat prickling his face. There was a kind of oven or furnace, its door open, bright flames glowing inside. A man stood there, in shirtsleeves, half of him lit by the glow. He wore a tough leather apron that went down past his knees. Hal and Czeszka joined the scattering of people who stood behind a barrier, watching respectfully, waiting for what must surely be magic to begin.

The man said that glass had been made for centuries. By accident, probably, at first. It was made of sand and ash.

Sand and ash and water that could come through the heat, purified into transparency. Glass was so hard that only a diamond could cut it.

Talking, he'd picked up a long wooden pole, metal-tipped. He dipped the end into a bucket and brought it out coated in shining liquid, like a sauce to eat with ice-cream. He held it into the furnace, turning it this way and that. Then he pulled it out, and showed how the tip had absorbed the fire's heat, glowing white, then flame-gold as it cooled. He began to twist and turn the pole in his hands, letting the molten glass sag into drips and runnels. Each time Hal thought a drop had become heavy enough to break free and fall, the man caught and twisted it into lightness again. He was making something that only he could see. Curves and spikes were forming, solidifying. It was no longer molten, but becoming glass: soft glass, still pliable, like melted sugar. With his hands holding the pole delicately, twisting, twirling, he was a conjuror, a magician, a dancer weaving shapes. When the piece was shaped to his satisfaction, he lifted it from the pole and held it out to show everyone. Czeszka sighed in admiration. He'd turned a shapeless blob into a sea-shell, a sea-shell made of glass.

Hal had never thought about how glass was made. If anyone had asked him, he'd have said it just *was*. Came out of the ground like that, and maybe people carved and polished it into shape. But sand, ash! Someone, for the first time ever, must have discovered that sand and ash could harden, turn clear. Someone had worked out how to do it, and do it again. Miraculous, it seemed.

'Is good, yes?' Czeszka touched his arm. 'Clever?'

'Mm.' As he turned to look at her he saw that Wesley

was standing behind him. He had the buggy, though his wife held the small girl in her arms to watch. Hal turned away quickly. He felt himself burning – from inside, not from the oven's heat. Unable to resist stealing another look, he saw Wesley bending to catch something the older girl said to him. As he turned his head so that she could speak directly into his ear, he gazed for a second straight at Hal. Surely he must recognise him, from the leisure centre?

The glassblower was starting a new piece. The molten glass was mixed with copper, to give a dark red colour. This time he blew at the glob through a long tube, making a bubble that would surely burst.

More people had come in, pushing towards the front. To watch, Hal would have to press closer, finding a gap. But all his attention was on Wesley now. He was tingled all through with pride, jabbed by anger. Wesley was the tallest person in the room; shining, he seemed to Hal, as if there was a glow from him as fierce as the heat from the furnace. All the light in the room was drawn to Wesley, gleaming off him, his eyes, his teeth, his skin. Couldn't everyone see?

If Wesley had registered Hal in that brief look, he made no sign. He was engrossed in the demonstration, and in his two little girls. A good father. A good father with his family.

Hal had the feeling that this ought to be different, that he could start again and *make* it different. He could stand here with Wesley behind him, Wesley's strength and tall-ness and blackness. He could half turn, and say, 'Look, Dad. Look at that.' And Wesley would call him Son, not Hal but Son, the way Osman's dad often called Osman Son. Wesley's arm would rest easily on Hal's shoulder.

It made his eyes hurt, thinking this. Something was growing and pressing inside him, forcing itself against his lungs and into his throat. He could hardly swallow or breathe. It was taking him over.

'Hal?' Czeszka was beside him, looking into his face, concerned. 'OK?' Her face seemed to swim at him from a distance. The room blurred; the flames in the furnace, the shadows leaping to the dark of the rafters. It felt like the middle of the night. He nodded, and turned away.

Now the glassblower held out the red goblet he'd made. There was clapping; he said, 'Thank you,' and gave a small bow, looking somehow more ordinary as fluorescent lights came on overhead, chasing away the darkness and the shadows. The demonstration was over, the spell broken. People were talking again, ending the silence that had held them while they watched in awe. They drifted away, towards the display cases, while Hal hung back to see what Wesley would do next. Valerie and the oldest girl, Vera, were soon exclaiming over some tiny glass sea-horses, arranged on weed-like ribbon to look as if they were underwater. Wesley had moved to one side, looking at coloured fisherman's floats on a mound of netting.

'For you!' Czeszka pulled at his arm, pointing excitedly. She drew him over to a stand on its own in the corner. Sand had been piled inside, heaped and then smoothed as if by a wave. And resting on it, beached there, were marbles – sea-coloured marbles, of deep green, turquoise-green, grey-green, some flecked with white like sea-foam. One was as large as a golf-ball, others small as pebbles. A spotlight inside the case made them gleam like precious jewels.

One in particular seemed to call to him: conker-sized,

with a swirl of the deepest green-blue as if a lifting wave was trapped there, the instant before it curled over and crashed to the beach. Its sea-light seemed directed at Hal, shining straight at him, dazzling him.

Wesley and marbles. Wesley and glass and marbles and sand, all here in the same room: confusing themselves, streaming into each other. Making and remaking, blurring and dissolving. It couldn't be coincidence, could it? Wesley liked marbles, so he'd brought his family here. He liked marbles because Tina Marborough had been his girlfriend. Mum. Marbles were a reminder of her. Marbles were his gift to Hal, his promise.

Hal was burning with expectation. He was scripting a scene in which Wesley would come and stand by him and gaze at that sea-green marble. Hal would say, 'I've still got them. The marbles you gave my mum.' And he'd take out the moon-marbles from his pocket – the lucky moon-marbles – and hold them in the palm of his hand. And Wesley would say – what? What next?

Hal was torn between an urge to grab Wesley by the arm, shake him and shout at him and force him to look and see and recognise, and a wish to get out, to run away. While he wavered, Wesley barely glanced at the display case before Vera called, 'Daddy! Look at these!' and tugged at his arm. She was excited by some glass cats, ugly and misshapen to Hal's eye. But Wesley went with her and bent down to examine the cats in great detail, asking Vera which one she liked best. Soon they went over to the counter, where pieces boxed and ready for sale were stacked up on shelves behind. Valerie and the smaller girl had chosen one of the tiny sea-horses. Wesley added one of the blue cats, and took out a twenty-pound note to pay for both.

'I'm going,' Hal told Czeszka abruptly. He pushed past the people waiting at the till, and went outside. The air was cool and fresh after the furnace heat and the press of people, but his eyes were burning and there was a dull, heavy pain in his chest.

Seeing Czeszka hurrying after him, he turned up the track towards the park railings and the promenade. He kicked at a stone and sent it ricocheting, then swiped at the railings, but succeeded only in bashing the side of his hand. The pain took a few moments to kick in, then he doubled up, swearing. A mother with toddlers pulled them hastily out of his path. Nursing his hand between his side and tucked elbow, he strode on faster, head down.

When his mobile started ringing in his pocket, jingling out its cheerful tune, he remembered Aunt Jude telling him to be back in time for early lunch. He had no idea what the time was, and assumed this must be her, but the name LUKE showed on the tiny screen. Purely from habit, he accepted the call. Why? Luke was the last person he wanted to talk to.

'What?' he snarled.

'Hey, Marbles, where are you?' Luke's voice sounded perfectly friendly, as if nothing had happened between them.

'Where d'you think? I'm in exile, remember?'

Huffed laughter, then: 'I know that, don't I? Lucky sod. But it's holidays now.'

'Yeah, but I'm still in Ryton.'

'Right. So am I. Where are you?'

'You're in—?'

'Here for half-term, aren't I?' said Luke's voice. 'Want to come sailing? Dad and I are going with this pal of his. He says you can come if you want.'

'Well, I *don't* want,' Hal rapped back.

'Oh, don't be wet – course you do. Meet us at—'

'No. I said no!' Hal ended the call and stuffed the mobile back in his pocket. His pace had slowed; he couldn't now remember where he was going, or why. Luke! Luke in Ryton! That's if he was telling the truth – it'd be just like Luke to wind him up by *pretending* to be here, when really he was at home. But then, why shouldn't he be in Ryton? His Dad had the caravan here. Still, that didn't mean Hal had to spend time with him.

Luke would be in the way.

Luke would crash in and spoil things.

Luke had a dad, a part-time dad he was always parading in Hal's face as if to emphasise what Hal hadn't got.

Luke meant trouble.

Worst of all, Luke brought out the side of Hal that *looked* for trouble.

The cry of a gull, very near, made him start. It was standing on top of a litter bin, and he was amazed at how huge it was, how sleek and white, with darker grey wings. He saw its sturdy pink legs, its webbed feet, its cunning yellow eye. It threw back its head and opened its bill wide in a loud, mocking wail that seemed directed at Hal.

'Wait, Hal!' It was Czeszka again, still in pursuit like a faithful dog. She'd gained on him while he paused to take the call. Now, caught in a tangle of wants and grudges, he let her approach.

'What's wrong?' She stood facing him squarely. 'That

man—' She gestured back towards the craft centre. 'You know him?'

'Yeah.' His eyes dropped. 'He's my dad.'

'Your—' He saw doubt flicker across Czeszka's face as she struggled to understand. 'Dad? Your father? But—'

'Yeah, I know. But. A great big But.'

He felt his face doing strange things, his mouth twisting into a sneer, his eyes stinging. He had to get away from her. The gull lifted itself into the air, balanced on the wind for a few moments, then flew off strongly.

'See you,' said Hal, not looking at Czeszka, and turned away along the sea-front.

14
SAIL

Don, Hal thought. He'd go to Don's beach hut. Don would be painting, or staring at the sea. Don wouldn't ask questions, wouldn't want to chat.

Again Hal's mobile jingled and trilled. Ready with a mouthful for Luke, Hal saw just in time that it was Aunt Jude's name on the screen.

'Hal, where are you?' She sounded cross. 'Are you on your way?'

'Yeah, OK,' he said, abandoning all idea of Don, of tossing stones, of watching the tide, of just being there. 'Five minutes.'

Aunt Jude was short with him when he got home. 'Half-past twelve, I said, Hal. I've had your lunch ready for nearly an hour. Where've you been?'

'Dunno,' he mumbled. 'Just out.'

'Much later and there won't be any point going.'

He looked at her blankly.

'To Sea Life! Had you forgotten? Don't you *want* to go?

I meant it as a treat for you, not a chore. Actually *I* want to go – I never have.'

She put his lunch on the table, omelette and salad. 'I've had mine. I got hungry waiting.'

The omelette had gone a bit leathery from being kept warm in the oven, and at first Hal thought he didn't want to eat anyway. When he jabbed at it, chopped ham and mushrooms slithered out from the creamy egg inside, and he realised how hungry he was, how his body needed food. With every mouthful, every swallow, he was gulping down his disappointment, taking it into himself.

He was just finishing, and Aunt Jude offering him a peach from the fruit-bowl, when the doorbell rang shrilly. Aunt Jude went to answer, returning after a few moments.

'For you. A surprise visitor.'

Wesley! It had to be. Come to apologise, to sort things out. Wesley on his own, without his wife and kids. Hal leapt up, sloshing fruit juice, knocking cutlery to the floor.

It was Luke who stood there in the hall, grinning broadly. Behind him – tall, filling all the space – was Graham, Luke's dad.

'Yess!' said Luke, and gave Hal's arm a friendly punch.

'Hi there, Hal,' said Graham.

Hal glared at Luke. 'How d'you know where to come?'

'Phone book. Marborough. Easy.'

'We've come to take you sailing,' said Graham. 'If you want, that is.'

Hal shook his head. 'Can't. We're going out.'

He was glad now of having Aunt Jude as an excuse, but to his dismay she said, 'No, I think we'll scrap it. We can go some other day. You don't want to miss the chance of sailing.'

'But I don't know how,' Hal mumbled. 'I've never done it.'

'No prob!' Luke's dad had a way of making everything seem easy. 'Luke's only been once before, haven't you, Luke? Mike knows what to do. He and Sarah – that's his wife – charter a yacht every year. He'll be in charge. Sarah's gone off with a friend for the day, so he can use a couple of strong lads to help out.'

'You'd like that, Hal, wouldn't you?' said Aunt Jude. 'What will he need?'

Hal opened his mouth to protest, but knew it would sound wet to say that he didn't want to. He *did*, as soon as he started thinking about it. Proper sailing, with the sky and the wind in his face! It was only Luke he didn't want.

He went to his room to fetch a sweatshirt and his padded coat. When he came down, Graham and Aunt Jude were exchanging mobile phone numbers, and Aunt Jude was saying, 'It'll be nice for him to have Luke's company after a whole week on his own.'

That showed how much *she* knew. But Hal decided to go along with it. Luke wouldn't be likely to start anything, not with his dad there.

'So,' said Luke in the car, turning round from the front seat, 'how's it been, your week off school?'

'Great. I mean, so boring I thought I'd die of it. But good as well.'

'What was so good, then?'

'Tell you later,' said Hal.

'Shame you had to miss Tuesday's match.'

'Yeah. Still, it was nice of you to text me the score. I really wanted to know about Greeny's hat-trick.'

Luke laughed delightedly. 'Winding you up! Durr! He didn't even play – sprained his ankle in practice.'

'You *what*?' Hal pretended to swipe him round the head.

Luke ducked forward, grinning, and added, 'Lee Briggs came on instead. We lost 2-1. Had you fooled, though, didn't I?'

'Wazzock!'

'If you two start fighting on the yacht,' Graham told them amiably, 'I'll chuck you both overboard.'

They were at the marina now; Graham found a place to park, and got a ticket from the machine. Walking down to the pontoons was like entering a world with its own rules and language and concerns. Hal had looked at sailing boats before, on his seaside outings with Mum: little sailing dinghies, and the bigger ocean going cruisers. He'd some times looked enviously at the people who moved around the decks or sat sipping drinks at their mooring. The freedom! Imagine being able to set sail and go wherever the wind and the tide took you!

Sleek yachts lined the pontoons like tethered racehorses. The clinking of rope-fastenings against masts made a cheerful, irregular rhythm. Mike – big and smiley like Luke's dad – was already on board a yacht called *Sunburst*. The others climbed over the guard rail and onto the deck.

'Good to have you along, Hal,' Mike said, and slapped him on the shoulder. 'Your first time? Don't worry – I'll show you the ropes.'

He meant it literally. A few minutes later, Hal, wearing a lifejacket and standing on the foredeck, had the job of letting slip the rope that held the front of the boat to the pontoon, while Luke did the same with the aft line. The engine was on, Graham at the helm, steering the yacht slowly back from its mooring, and round into the channel that led to the open sea. People were watching from the railings above, and Hal knew that they envied him, as he'd envied people he'd seen on boats before – their skill, their confidence, which he now pretended to have, as if he did this all the time. He and Luke pulled in the fenders, the large balloon-shaped floats that protected the side of the boat from knocks, and stowed them under the bench that ran round the cockpit.

The yacht moved slowly through the harbour entrance and well clear of the buoys, and now came the exciting business of hoisting the sails. Hal's job was to tighten the rope called the main sheet, at first hauling and then using a winch. Above him, with a thrilling ripple of canvas, the sail unconcertinaed itself to reach up the mast. When it was adjusted and tight to the wind, the headsail was unfurled, using ropes on each side. Both sails tautened, streamers fluttering from their edges. Mike told Graham to turn off the engine, and now they were *sailing,* nothing but the wind powering the yacht through the waves. 'Woo-hoo!' shouted Luke, as the deck tipped and tilted beneath their feet. Hal looked across at him and they exchanged grins.

The shore receded fast; when Hal turned his head, he could just make out the line of beach huts, with stunted trees behind. You saw differently from here. What was important was the sea, grey and choppy, the boat dipping into it, riding the waves like a gull; the marker-posts and buoys, and fast-scudding speedboats, and yachts whose paths might cross yours, and a big container-ship Graham said was heading for Portsmouth. The land was irrelevant;

nothing mattered except the sails and the wind and the tide. *Sunburst* and its crew were a team; everyone had something to do. If you weren't at the helm, Mike said, or checking the course, you were on lookout.

Luke steered for a while; then Mike surprised Hal by offering him a turn, too.

Hal fitted himself behind the helm, which was the size of a bicycle wheel. Mike showed him what to do; how to keep a light touch, always adjusting and correcting. 'That's it. That's it. Don't over-steer or we'll go wallowing all over the place.'

Sunburst felt like a live thing, a horse impatient to gallop, bucking and tilting under his feet, the prow plunging and rising, throwing up bursts of spray. The wind freshened, and soon the yacht was heeling over to starboard, tilted at what seemed an alarming angle. Hal felt he was barely in control, but still Mike was by his elbow, quite calm, saying, 'That's it. That's right. Bring her up into the wind. Bit more. Good lad.'

He was doing something right! Doing it for the first time and not doing too badly at all. Doing at least as well as Luke had.

'You've got a good touch, for a first-timer,' Mike told him. And for a few moments he left Hal on his own, while he went down into the saloon to fetch cold drinks from the fridge. Later, while Graham took over the steering, Mike showed the boys the tiny cabins fore and aft, the compact kitchen, and how the table could be folded away to make more sleeping space. Hal was more interested in the little screen that showed satellite mapping of their position. He wouldn't mind learning more about that.

By the time the sails were lowered and the yacht slipping

cleanly back to her mooring, Hal felt he'd been on a voyage quite away from his ordinary life. His face burned from sun and spray; he could taste salt when he licked his lips, and his skin felt clammed with it. His hands and face were cold, but underneath he was warmed with effort and pride. He'd done something new, and had learned at least the very first things about sailing.

'Well done, lads,' said Mike, last to step down to the pontoon, once the boat was made fast, everything checked, and the hatch locked up.

Hal remembered to say thank you. 'It was great. Well cool.'

'My pleasure,' Mike told him. 'Come again, you and Luke, any time. Get Graham to give me a call if you're at a loose end.'

The four of them went to a nearby fish-and-chip restaurant and tucked into big platefuls of battered plaice, mushy peas and chips. They dolloped brown sauce and picked out the hair-like bones and cleared a whole plateful of bread and butter. It was the best meal Hal had eaten for ages.

Anyone looking at the four of them, it struck him, might have supposed they were two dads and two sons. It wasn't hard to tell that Graham and Luke were father and son; they had the same short thick hair, the same straight noses and wide grins. But anyone mistaking Mike for Hal's father would have had to picture a black mother, a reversal of the real situation.

When they'd finished, Graham paid the bill, saying that this was his treat. The two men went off for a drink at the Anchor, and Luke and Hal wandered back to the marina. Already Hal felt a wave of regret that the afternoon of sea and wind and sail was over. He could do it again, Mike had said so. But for that to happen, he had to be friends with Luke.

And this was too easy, as if they'd never quarrelled; they'd slipped back into being friends again. Part of Hal was glad, and part was resentful. It shouldn't be so easy. Luke should back down, say he'd got it all wrong. He ought to grovel.

'So,' Luke said, 'how's it going with the old geezer? The grandad?' He gave Hal a meaningful look that brought back all the taunts, all the bad feeling. Hal felt himself prickling.

'Not there, is he?' Hal scuffed his shoe on the ground. 'Gone to Spain. I wouldn't be here if he was around.'

'Racist git,' Luke spat out.

'Yeah?' Hal looked at him. 'You'd know all about that.'

'Uh?'

'Come on! It's you that's racist.'

Luke stopped dead. '*Me*? How d'you work that out?'

'The things you *said*. The things you kept going on about.'

'What things?'

'You know! About my grandad. About my mum. Even about my dad. You don't know the first thing about him, but that didn't stop you having a go.'

'Don't be stupid!' Luke gave an impatient laugh. 'It's not like *I* think those things! I was just saying.'

'Yeah, well *don't* say. Keep your scuzzy ideas to yourself.' Hal's fists were clenching; his jaw clamped tight. It was no use thinking he could be friends with Luke. Ever.

'Cool it, OK? Just cool it!' Luke was saying. 'You've got it all wrong. I knew you had, only you wouldn't listen. All I said was your *grandad*'s a racist. And he is, he must be!

You've said so, loads of times. If *I* was, I'd hardly be best mates with you and Oz, would I?'

'But my dad. You said my dad might be a racist. Didn't want me cos – I'm not properly black.'

It hurt, physically hurt, to say it. Did that mean it was true? He had to close his eyes and spit it out, like something that had been lodged in his throat, choking him. And immediately he wished he hadn't.

Luke looked at him, seemed about to speak, stopped. He scuffed his feet, tried again. 'Yeah. Yeah, I did say that. OK, I shouldn't have. It was just a thought. Look, forget it, can you? Forget I opened my big mouth. Mates?' He turned, holding up a hand towards Hal in a high five.

Hal didn't respond until Luke made a comical pleading face.

'Oh, go on then. Mates.' Hal held up his own palm to strike Luke's. ' 'Cept I've been excluded, and you haven't.'

'Yeah, right. You've had a free week's holiday.'

Hal laughed. 'Yeah. It's been great.'

'Boring as hell, you said!'

'I know. I'm winding you up.'

They'd reached the railings that formed the boundary of the marina. Luke climbed onto the top one, supporting himself with one hand on a lamp-post, and mimed looking out to sea through a telescope.

'There's something else.' Hal found himself saying it before he'd even decided to. 'I've seen my dad. I know who he is.'

'Whoa! You're kidding me!' Luke pretended to over-balance, windmilling his arms to stop himself toppling over.

'I'm not. I saw him today. And I'm meeting him again tomorrow. He's really cool.'

'Hey, can I come? We're not doing much tomorrow. Dad's playing golf – *boring* – but I don't have to go. What time? Where?'

'No. Can't.' Hal was already backing off. 'Not yet. Maybe later. Look, I ought to get back.'

Luke was staring at him, still perched high. Hal called, 'Catch you later,' and set off at a jog, his mind blurring all over again.

Why had he said that? Why hadn't he told Luke the truth, instead of adding that stupid lie?

15
TOMORROW

He'd had it with pretending. With waiting. Waiting for what? Now that he knew who his father was, he had to *do* something.

He'd reached the fork in the road and the bottom end of Laurel Drive, but instead of turning left he continued straight, as far as the gravel alleyway that led down to the beach. Aunt Jude hadn't said what time he had to be in – she'd left it up to Graham.

Would Don still be at the hut? It was possible; he sometimes stayed out late. Don wouldn't quiz him about the sailing, the way Aunt Jude would. You could just *be*, with Don, not needing to chat unless you felt like it. Find Don. Find Don. His feet beat out the rhythm as he pounded along the walkway.

There were no street lights here, but Hal liked the feeling of being out alone in the dark, under the sky. The tide was in. At high tide the sea seemed so different: savage, beating and crashing onto the shingle as if intent on gnawing it away. The moon, behind shifting clouds, glimmered silverily on the sea and gave enough light to see where he was walking. Ahead were the outlines of the beach huts, their pointed roofs, moonlight reflecting in their windows. Most were locked and empty, some already closed up for winter. But brightness lit Don's open door, and – yes! – there he was, in a yellow raincoat that made him look like lifeboat crew, sitting in a wicker chair on the deck, smoking. Not painting, not sketching, Hal saw as he came closer – just smoking, and gazing out to sea. Hal saw the glow of the cigarette-tip.

Don didn't turn as he approached, didn't even seem to hear his footsteps. For a moment, Hal thought something was wrong; then Don seemed to come to himself. He gave a slow smile, and said, 'Hal,' as if he'd been expecting him. He was well wrapped-up against the evening's cool, with a sweater underneath the raincoat, though as usual his ankles and bony shins showed in the gap between socks and cut-off trousers.

'Didn't know you smoked,' Hal said lightly.

'I do sometimes, only not in the house. She won't have it. Says I'm crazy to fill my lungs with tar, and there's no arguing with that. Where you off to, then?'

'I'm not. I came to find you.'

'Did you? – nngg.' Don seemed pleased. 'I'm not very good company. Not today.'

Hal said nothing. He sat on the doorstep and stretched out his legs. Don didn't have to be good company. He could just be himself.

'Have you been painting?' Hal asked.

Don shook his head and drew at his cigarette. 'No, not really. Couldn't get going. It's like that sometimes. You've got to have bad days to get the good ones. But that doesn't make the bad days any better. I'm a painter, so if I can't paint, what am I? Complete waste of space, that's what. Completely sick of myself.' He stretched out his arms and legs, made them rigid, tilted his head back. 'I'd better shut up shop. It's late. She'll be – kuh – wondering where I am. Where you are, too.' He began to get stiffly to his feet.

'Wait!' said Hal. 'I want to ask you something.'

'Go on then.' Don settled again, and looked at him expectantly.

Hal looked down at the decking, where fine grains of sand had blown against the doorstep. He pinched some together, let them trickle from his fingers. 'It's about my dad.'

Don gave no response, bending to stub out his cigarette underneath his plimsoll.

'My dad,' Hal said, more emphatically. 'I've seen him. He's here in Ryton.'

'Uh-huh.'

'You *know*, don't you?' Hal looked at him, waiting for a reaction. 'Aunt Jude told you. I heard her. She saw him, didn't she? *Met* him. Only she didn't tell me. No one tells me anything. It's not fair.'

'No,' said Don. He reached into his canvas bag for another cigarette and a matchbox, and lit up. Hal took this as encouragement; Don wasn't going to end the conversation and hurry away. He caught the sulphur tang of the match, and a waft of cigarette-smoke.

'So,' he appealed, 'what should I do? I know it's him – Wesley Prince. That's why my mum calls me Prince Hal, isn't it? And then there's the marbles—' He felt in his pocket.

'What marbles?'

'Here's one.' Hal held it out, his favourite, the one with the smoky-blue swirl. 'He gave Mum a bag of them, and she gave them to me – and today, just today, there he was, Wesley, my dad, looking at glass stuff in this workshop place, and marbles. It proves it, doesn't it?'

Don only looked puzzled. Hal tried again.

'Aunt Jude – when she told you about Wesley, told you she'd met him – she said he was my father, didn't she? She must have told you that!'

Don nodded slowly. 'Yes. Yes, she did. But—'

'Only – I don't think he knows. He's seen me twice now, but he doesn't recognise me. What should I do? It's no good asking *her* – she won't help. All she says is wait and ask Mum. But Mum won't tell me anything either. I don't need to know, that's what she always says when I ask. *Don't need to know!* It's doing my head in!'

'Well, you're asking the wrong person.' Don gazed out at the sea. 'How can *I* help? Who am I to tell you what to do? I've – kuh! – messed up my own life, made a right pig's ear of it, let alone sort out anyone else's. Ask Jude. Ask your mum. Ask anyone, only not me. Ask this Wesley. Ask him. He ought to know.'

Hal clutched this to him. There was a silence. What Don had said seemed to require a response, so he made himself ask, 'Messed up how? I mean, you're famous. You're on Google.'

Don gave a snorting laugh and a twitch that jolted the cigarette right out of his hand. Hal scrabbled to pick it up and hand it back.

'*Famous!*' Don scoffed. 'That doesn't mean anything. It's just fashion. In one minute, out the next. The world doesn't know what's good and what's rubbish, only what's shoved in its face. Trouble is, I was sucked in by it. The praise, the attention, the publicity. I was that stupid. Couldn't see how worthless it all was.'

'Sucked in how?'

Don puffed out smoke. 'Started to think they must be right. I must be doing something really good. And it was – kuh! – a short step from there to thinking *everything* I did had to be amazing. I must be a genius.'

'But – that wouldn't mess up your whole life, would it?' Hal said. 'I mean, lots of people think they're cool – footballers, singers, film stars.'

'No, but when I say messed up, I mean I *messed up*,' Don insisted. 'Chuck – k – chucked it all away. D'you know when I was happiest?'

'No,' Hal said. Of course he didn't.

Don looked at him. 'When I was struggling. When I didn't know if I was any good or not, but I was trying my damnedest. Before I was successful, whatever successful means.' He paused. 'I was married, then. Had a little boy. Jake. I was happy. We all were. We lived in a flat in Fulham, with an attic for me to paint in. But then I got *famous*.' He sneered the word. 'And I couldn't handle it. I was forever being invited to parties and art shows; I won prizes; I was in the papers. I thought all my birthdays had come at once. I lapped it up – the drink, the girls, the money – more of everything than I could possibly want. I didn't see, not till it was – kkk! – too late, that I was throwing away my marriage. She left me, and took Jake with her.'

'She?' echoed Hal. 'You're not talking about Aunt Jude?'

Of course not; there was no Jake that he'd heard of. But

the question sent Don into a fit of croaking laughter that almost tipped him off his chair. 'No! No. Not Jude. She'd have sorted me out, no problem. No, she came along much later. Picked me up, dusted me down, set me on my feet again. Made me think my life was worth living after all. But I'd lost Jake, lost my boy, and Cindy – that's my wife. *Was* my wife. Too late to get them back.'

'But can't you see him if you want to? Don't you have rights?'

'He's a grown man now, Hal. Forty next birthday. Kids of his own. So it's up to him whether he sees me or not – lets me see *them* – and he chooses not. Cindy married again, and Jake's closer to his step-dad. He sees me out of duty, couple of times a year, and sends me news of the grandkids. But I could have had a proper family if I hadn't been so damned stupid. If I could go back, Hal, I'd do things differently, believe me. Trouble is, you never can. See, I told you I'm no use to anyone. Waste of space.'

Hal wanted to say *You're not,* but couldn't get the words out.

Don seemed to take his silence as confirmation. 'Well. So. There we are. You don't want to listen to me blathering on.' He seemed suddenly embarrassed at having said so much. He got stiffly to his feet and lifted the wicker chair inside the hut, then tidied the brushes and pencils on the table. 'But it's a crying shame to see these rifts in families – these arguments that go on and on till it's too late.'

'Like with my grandad,' Hal said.

'Yes. It's not your doing, but put it right if you can.' Don hesitated. 'And – find your Wesley, tell him who you are.'

'Is that what you think?'

'Yes! Do a bit of mending.' Don came out and locked the door. 'Come on. Let's get back while we can still see one foot in front of the other. We'll be in trouble, this rate.'

Don was right about that: Aunt Jude was annoyed with both of them.

'Hal, it's thoughtless of you, going off like that! I phoned Graham and he said you'd set off home an hour ago. And why didn't you have your mobile turned on? As for you—' She rounded on Don. 'Keeping him out so late without telling me – I despair of you sometimes! What a pair – bad as each other, you are!'

But her crossness was soon over. She made hot chocolate, and Welsh rarebit for Don, who hadn't eaten since lunchtime. She asked Hal about the sailing, and told them she'd made some progress with the sale of Marborough's, so had spent the time usefully.

When Hal went upstairs to bed, and thought of everything that had happened since morning, it seemed enough to fill several days. Now he felt buoyed up by his decision.

Tomorrow. Tomorrow he'd find Wesley and tell him.

Before turning off his bedside light, he reached for his bag of marbles. He put the two moons back in, and thought of letting himself choose, for such an important day, instead of picking at random as he usually did.

But which would be best? Which would bring more luck? The tiger-eye? The orange one that he used to think would taste of fizzy orange if he put it in his mouth? The black one flecked with silver?

No – he needed a bigger than usual amount of luck. He'd take the whole bag.

16
PROOF

Hal was awake early, full of purpose.

Today. The Day.

He drew his curtains and looked out at the garden. The sky was grey and tousled, unsettled. But still it was The Day. The Day that would be the start of everything being different.

His main worry now was that Aunt Jude would have plans for him. When he went downstairs she was already up, dressed in her red sweater and black jeans. She never seemed to drift around the house in a dressing-gown, with the newspaper and a mug of tea, the way Mum often did on a Sunday. Busy and active from the moment she got up, that was Aunt Jude. She was adjusting the time on the dining-room clock.

'Have you remembered to put your watch back an hour?' she called to Hal. 'It's only half-past seven, not half-past eight.'

A day with an extra hour in it! It seemed a good omen.

Hal turned back the hands on his watch. Aunt Jude

came into the kitchen and started fiddling with the cooker clock. 'I'll get breakfast as soon as I've done this,' she told him. 'I was thinking about our Sea Life trip. You could ask Luke if he wants to come. Would you like that?'

Dismay clutched at Hal's throat. 'Today?'

'Tomorrow, I thought. I need to do some garden-tidying while the weather's reasonable. I want it to look good for when your grandad comes home. Feel like helping?'

'Uh. I need to go out first.'

Aunt Jude looked at him.

'I want to get a present for Mum,' he improvised. Well, maybe he would.

'Oh, that's a nice idea. But why not wait till tomorrow and get something at Sea Life? They're bound to have a gift shop there.'

'No,' Hal insisted. 'I saw something yesterday. At a glass-blowing place.'

She nodded. 'I know where you mean. Well, take your coat – it's turned colder today. And be back by one o'clock. *One o'clock*, OK? And leave your mobile *on*. I thought I'd do proper Sunday lunch.'

Hal left as soon as he'd finished breakfast. The free hours beckoned, full of promise. He jogged down Laurel Drive, slowing when he saw Don coming the other way, in his yellow raincoat and a saggy green hat.

'You're late!' Hal greeted him.

'You're early! Where are you rushing off to?'

Hal didn't want to say it. '*You* know.'

Don touched his arm, then twitched away. 'Hal, I've been thinking. Maybe it's not such a good idea. Maybe you should wait.'

'*Wait*? But you said—'

'I know I did. But I shouldn't have. It's going to be a big shock, isn't it, for this Wesley? Maybe you should talk to your mum first.'

'But I *have* talked to her.' Hal heard his voice, impatient and whining like a little kid's. 'I've asked and asked. She won't tell me a single thing.'

'Still. You could wait just a bit longer.'

Disappointed beyond words, Hal said nothing. He couldn't speak, couldn't swallow. He'd thought Don was on his side.

Don looked at him quizzically, and added, 'Huh? Nnng.'

'Huh? Nnng,' Hal went back, exaggerating Don's twitch.

He shouldn't have. But he'd done it, and seen Don's hurt expression. It made Hal feel good. And it made him feel bad.

'See you later,' he called, and was already past and running.

He wasn't changing his mind. Not now.

The leisure centre: he'd try there first. It was barely eight o'clock, but most sports centres opened early.

Slung over one shoulder was his rucksack, with little in it but the bag of marbles. He heard their faint chink and grate as he ran. At first he'd put them in his hoodie pocket, but the whole bagful was too bulky; then he thought he'd just carry them, but felt too conspicuous – people might notice. They were too secret to carry openly for anyone to see.

He ran and jogged all the way, but as he neared the entrance his feet slowed. He saw parked cars, and the foyer doors standing open. His heart was pounding; his hands felt clammy. Desperately he hoped Wesley would be at work; it would be easier to speak to him here than if he were at home with his family. Did Wesley work weekends? He'd been off yesterday, but maybe he did Sundays. Someone had to.

There was no Wesley at the desk – just a bored-looking ginger-haired woman, leaning sideways and picking at a fingernail.

Hal's eyes went swimmy. It took a few moments for them to focus on the plaque on the wall behind, DUTY MANAGER: WESLEY PRINCE.

Gathering the frayed threads of his determination, Hal went up to the counter.

'Is Wesley Prince around?' he asked, in the most casual voice he could produce.

The woman barely glanced at him, then brought out a printed list from under the desk. 'Yeah, he's around some-where. There was a problem at the pool. Try over there.'

'Which way's that?'

With just a hint of a smirk, she pointed to a sign to his right: SWIMMING POOL. PLAY POOL.

Following the arrows, Hal found himself entering a changing area: rows of lockers, cubicles; through an arch, a glimpse of turquoise-blue, and the flailing arms of length-swimmers. He smelled chlorine and shampoo. A dad ushered two small boys towards the play-pool steps, and an infant waddled in front of Hal, plump hands clutching at an inflatable ring round its waist.

Hal went through the arch, ignoring a sign that said NO OUTDOOR CLOTHES OR FOOTWEAR BEYOND THIS POINT. A pool-guard's high chair stood at the deep end, with a teenage boy perched on top, and next to it stood Wesley. Both wore track pants and polo shirts in leisure centre colours. Wesley was saying something to the boy; both of them were watching the pool. The water reflected the ceiling lights in a blue shimmer; clean and tame, it looked, now that Hal was used to the sea.

Hal walked over the wet tiles between the play-pool and the main one. It felt weird being fully dressed in a place where swim-trunks and costumes were the norm.

'Whoa there!' Wesley came towards him, holding up a hand, barring him. 'You can't come in here dressed like that! Didn't you see the sign? Back to the changing rooms, please.' His eyes held Hal's for a moment in puzzlement. Surely, surely he recognised him?

'I've got to talk to you,' Hal told him, in a hoarse whisper that tried to exclude the other boy.

Wesley's eyebrows rose. 'To me? Fine, only not here. If you go back to reception I'll be right with you.'

'No,' Hal said urgently. 'Not at reception. It's private. Personal.'

A brief glance, a *search me* look, flicked between Wesley and the pool-guard. Then Wesley gave a slight shrug, and walked beside Hal along the length of the pool, past the showers and lockers and cubicles, and out to the corridor.

There Wesley stopped. 'How can I help you?' He smiled and nodded at someone hurrying by; he wasn't giving Hal his whole attention. Not yet.

Knowing that he knew more than Wesley, that he held the surprise and therefore the power, made Hal feel bold.

'I'm your son,' he said clearly.

Wesley did a double-take, a real double-take: his eyes seemed to waver, then refocus on Hal's face.

'Wh—' He stopped, swallowed. '*What?*'

'Your son,' Hal repeated, looking at him closely.

'How – how d'you work that out?'

Hal felt dizzy; the walls and ceilings of the corridor reeled around him. That was as good as *yes*, wasn't it?

Wesley was staring at him. 'Who are you? You were here the other day, weren't you? And yesterday at the Crafts Centre?'

'I'm Hal.'

'Hal . . . ?' Wesley prompted.

'Hal Marborough.'

That was the word that cut through Wesley's blankness, made his eyes widen and his mouth open. How perfect his teeth were, how white and strong.

'Marborough! So your mother's—'

'Tina Marborough.'

'Tina! You're Tina's boy! And she told you—' Wesley lowered his voice, his face incredulous '—she told you I'm your father?'

There. He'd *said* it. So it was true, beyond doubt.

'No, she didn't say. I worked it out.'

Wesley held up a flat hand, just as he'd done at the poolside: *Stop. No more.* 'We can't talk about this here. Come with me.'

Hal's step was light as he followed Wesley back towards the foyer. *I'm your father.* Wesley had said it. *Said* it! OK, he didn't look delighted, nor thrilled – but that could come later, when he'd got used to the idea. Told his wife.

Wesley led the way into a small office with a desk, coffee-table and low chairs. He gestured to Hal to sit, and took the other chair, leaving the door open. Then he sat forward, elbows on knees, and looked intently at Hal.

He seemed to think carefully for a few moments. Then:

'I'm not your father. I don't know what gave you that idea, but I'm definitely not.' He spoke not unkindly, but firmly.

'But you just said you *were!*' Hal burst out.

'I didn't! I asked why you thought I was. Tina didn't say so, did she? Surely not. It's years and years since I've seen her – the last I knew, she was at university. How old are you, Hal?'

'Thirteen. Fourteen in January.'

Wesley sat back. 'So you were born in – uh, ninety-five? Yes?'

Hal nodded.

'Well – I haven't seen Tina since – um, let me think – ninety-*three*. October ninety-three. So you see, it's impossible. Your father must be someone she met later – at university, perhaps.'

Dates and numbers whirled in Hal's brain. 'It's not impossible! Look, I've got proof – these—'

He grappled with the clip fastenings of his rucksack, then fumbled inside. Triumphantly, he produced the bag of marbles, and held it out to Wesley with both hands.

'What's this?'

'Look!' Hal pulled open the drawstring fastening, and shook the bag to make the marbles chink. He reached in and took one out – yes, the tiger's eye! – to hold up, in case there could be any doubt at all.

Wesley only looked baffled. 'Sorry, you've lost me.'

'Oh, come on! You gave them to Mum, didn't you? Because people called her Marbles, same as I get called. And she told me they were from my father.'

Wesley looked at the marbles and then at Hal, shaking his head slowly. 'Sorry, no. Maybe they *are* from your father, but not from me. Yes, I called her Marbles sometimes – people did – but I didn't give these to Tina. I've never seen them before.'

'You're lying!' Hal burst out. 'I know you are!'

There was pity now in the way Wesley looked at him: pity and concern. And it didn't look like concern for his *son* – just a stranger's sympathy for a weird kid who was throwing a strop. This, even more than denial, fuelled Hal's anger. He tried to say more, but it came out as a strangled gulp.

'Hal, please believe me. I'm not lying,' said Wesley, in a voice of quiet reasonableness. 'I'm sorry if you're disappointed. Obviously you want to know who your father is, but it's not me. Truthfully it isn't. I'm married to Valerie and we've got two little girls of our own. Before that – quite a while before – I went out with your mum. We were both teenagers when we met. I liked her a lot and we had good times together, and I was sorry when we split up. She was the one who ended it. She went off to Manchester and I went to Loughborough to do sports management. We both met new people, lost touch. That's it. I didn't even know she'd had a baby. How is she, anyway?'

'She's in hospital,' Hal spat out. Immediately he

remembered that Mum was at Claire's now, but he didn't tell Wesley that.

'Oh, I'm sorry,' Wesley said. 'You're having a tough time, aren't you?'

Hal huffed a laugh. 'Yeah. You could say that.'

Wesley's scrutiny was making him feel big and awkward. His eyes were stinging and his face felt puffy, his head throbbing enough to burst. His limbs felt uncontrollable, as if they might lash out, kick and hit. He wanted to hit Wesley. Snatching at his rucksack, he stuffed the bag of marbles back in, spilling some on the floor, where they rolled noisily. He'd have walked out without them, but Wesley gathered them up, scrabbling under his chair, and handed them back. Hal looked at the three marbles cupped in the palm of Wesley's hand; he fumbled, trying to take them, and almost dropped them again. Time seemed to have gone into slow-motion. His fingers felt like a bunch of bananas, but at last he'd got them, thrust them in with the others.

He was on his feet, blundering towards the open door. Wesley stood in his way, putting a restraining hand on his arm. Hal could easily have hit out. He pushed roughly back, but Wesley was a big man, strong and fit, and probably trained in karate or something. With no effort at all he deflected Hal's arm so that the shove twisted uselessly to one side.

'Let go!' Hal bleated, though Wesley had never grabbed hold.

'Now, look,' Wesley said, in a low, infuriatingly calm voice. 'You've got yourself upset. I can't let you leave like this. Who's looking after you? Is there someone I can phone? Someone who can come and fetch you?'

'Piss off!' Hal hissed it through clenched teeth. He ducked past Wesley and out, ignoring another male staff member who was approaching the door, drawn by the shouting.

Hal ran.

17

MOONY

Wesley was lying. Hal knew he had to be.

Lying. Wesley. Wesley. Lying.

The words banged and hammered in Hal's head while his feet pounded the pavement.

Wesley. Liar. Liar. Wesley.

Drumming and thumping. His feet trying to outrun the voice in his brain.

Had to be lying. Nothing made sense, otherwise.

Either that, or he'd got the dates wrong. Thirteen years, fourteen – it was a long time ago. How could he be so *sure*?

Hal didn't know where he was going, or where he wanted to be. Only that he had to be away from everyone. Had to think. Had to not think. Didn't want to be with his thoughts. Didn't want to be with himself.

One thing he *was* sure of – Wesley hadn't known about him. Hadn't known his name, hadn't known he existed. Wesley's surprise had been genuine; he hadn't been faking.

Mum had ended it. Wesley had said so.

Because she was pregnant? Pregnant, and hadn't told Wesley?

But the dates—

Wesley must have got it wrong. Mum had been pregnant, so she'd dumped him.

Why? Why would she? Wouldn't Wesley be the person she'd want to be with?

He was arguing himself into knots and tangles.

There was only one person who knew. And he could ask her now. His mobile was in his pocket.

Reaching the road, he turned left instead of right towards the town and sea-front, then left again into a builder's yard. A truck was parked there, alongside stacks of wooden pallets, broken slabs and a heap of gravel. Nettles and brambles grew thickly by a mesh fence.

He shrugged off his rucksack, dropped it on the ground and took his mobile out of his pocket. When he rang Mum's number she answered almost at once.

'Hal!' He could hear the smile in her voice. 'How are you? How was the sailing? I bet it was great.'

'Fine. Mum—'

'Is everything all right? Are you with Aunt Jude?'

'No. Yeah. I've just been talking to Wesley Prince.'

A beat's silence. Then: '*Wesley Prince*? What – how – is he there at the house?'

'No. But Mum – is Wesley my dad? Is he?'

Another pause, then: 'No, Hal, he isn't. What's happened? How did you meet him? What made you think—?'

No, Hal, he isn't.

No, Hal, he isn't.

His last hope, gone.

'But—' he whimpered. 'Are you sure?'

'Hal, of course I'm sure. Wesley was my boyfriend, but he's not your father. Definitely not.'

There was a silence. Hopelessness crashed around Hal, beat in his ears, muffled his throat. Back where he was. Dadless. Fatherless. Wesleyless. No nearer knowing than he'd ever been. He stared around, at the nettles, the brambles, some bits of chip paper caught in the fence; he'd forgotten he was still connected, until Mum started speaking again.

'Hal? Hal? Are you still there?'

'Yeah,' he said, not feeling as if he was.

'Listen. I'm coming down to see you. I'll tell you – a bit more, OK? You need to know. Only thing is, I can't drive, so I'll have to wait till Claire can bring me. Where are you now?'

'Uh – I'm—'

'Are you at the house? Is Aunt Jude there?'

Impossible to speak, to give a sensible reply. He ended the call, and switched off his mobile. Then he tore at the nettles, grasping a handful of stalks together, tearing off the leaves. The stinging and prickling of his palms was almost pleasurable. Picking up half a brick, he flung it as hard as he could, and watched it bounce and skitter off the rutted concrete. Then he ran up the slope of gravel, his feet slithering. He kicked and trampled the heap, fell on his hands and knees, got up again, stamped out his fury and frustration. Tears ran down his face and into the sides of his mouth.

How pathetic he must look! A big kid having a tantrum. There might be security cameras. Dogs patrolling.

He picked up his rucksack and slunk away.

Now he remembered that he'd told Luke. Czeszka, too.

A stupid boast, that's all it had been. He'd made a prat of himself, and soon they'd know.

The town seemed too small now, small and suffocating. He thought everyone he saw would stare at him, would guess how stupid he'd been. He felt like a little lost boy who might burst into tears. Hurrying – but why? What for? What was the use of anything, now? – he was soon at the sea-front, facing the beach. Below a grey sky the wind was strengthening, gusting in from the sea. Some way out he saw a sailing-boat making way with difficulty, bobbing and rocking. The waves were white-topped, which meant rough weather, as Hal knew from his sailing trip. White horses, Mike had called them; Hal remembered that with a distant, irrelevant part of his mind. A dog-walker passed him and called out a cheery 'good morning'. His dog, a spaniel, barked and barked at the waves, dashing back as each one rolled in.

Hal felt in a mood to be angered by anyone who seemed pointlessly happy. Some people seemed cheerful merely to be alive. Mum, sometimes. Aunt Jude, definitely. Hal wanted gloom. He wanted rain and thunder and fog. He wanted everyone to be as miserable as he was.

Mum, he knew, would be straight on the phone to Aunt Jude. They'd be talking about him, whispering the things he mustn't know, the things they knew but weren't going to tell him. As if he was a little kid, too young or too dim to be told the truth.

He hated them. Hated everyone.

He hurled a boulder into the sea, then another – grazing his fingers and his knuckles as he heaved them up, getting sand and grit under his nails and into the small cuts and grazes he was giving himself. The *dunk* of each stone going in, the explosion of water, gave him brief satisfaction, but then he was restless again, looking for another, bigger one. Bigger and bigger. Heavy enough for his resentment. Heavy enough to make a tsunami.

Half of him, the Wesley half, the half he thought he'd found, the Jamaican half, the half with a kindly grandfather and a family and a place, had faded again, been washed into the sea, dissolved, gone, had left him stranded and alone, had never been part of him at all.

When he tired of chucking stones, he stood panting. What now?

Don. This had to be Don's fault, didn't it? Don had *told* him to go and see Wesley, *told* him, yes, Wesley was his father. Sort it out, he'd said.

He jogged along the row of beach huts expecting to see Don sitting on the deck, or going down to swim, or his hut door fastened open while he sat inside painting.

The hut was locked up like all the others. Not a sign of him.

But Don was *always* here. Hal had taken it for granted that he'd be here now. Don had to be the one to receive his anger: Mum was too far away, his father still invisible. Don was the only one within reach.

He could go in anyway. He knew where Don put the key – underneath the big stone beside the door. Brainless! Moronic! Wasn't that the first place anyone would think of looking?

And there it was.

Hal unlocked the door, hooked it back and went in.

The hut smelled of white spirit and coffee and dampness. Everything was just as Don had left it: the table covered with a litter of paint tubes and brushes, pencil stubs, an empty cigarette packet, sticks of charcoal, articles torn from newspapers, a leaflet about the new Arts Centre, postcards, sketches, nails and screws, several pound coins and odd bits of change, a mug with dregs of sticky brown, an envelope addressed to Don Inchbold, a Stanley knife with a sharp blade, half a Kit-Kat, stones and shells from the beach, a roll of parcel tape.

Next to the table stood the easel with a painting propped on it, on a rectangle of the Daler board Don used. There was a layer of pale wash and some darker shapes, underneath an angry scribble of charcoal. Hal remembered Don's bad day – was the charcoal a scrawling-over of failed work, or part of the picture?

The bottom part of the table was made of two large shelves, each as large as the table-top. Flat boards were stacked there, dozens of them, some swathed in plastic, or cardboard or bubble-wrap. Hal hesitated. He wanted to shout at Don, rage at him, tell him he was stupid, he'd got it all wrong about Wesley, he'd lied. But he felt daunted by the atmosphere of the hut. He shouldn't have come in while Don wasn't there.

Shrugging off doubt, he knelt on the floor and pulled at the stack of pictures on the lower shelf. Boards and plastic slid and tilted to the floor. Reckless now, Hal tugged at the shelf above, producing another satisfying slither.

Painting after painting after painting. Various sizes and styles; some were the merest breath on the board, like the first wisp of an idea, hardly captured; others were finished and signed. Some were mounted and framed, others just raw-edged board. Most startling of all was that several had big letters slashed across them in bright red:

USELESS
RUBBISH
CRAP

Hal laid these out in a row on the sofa, and stared at them. Bad days? Don's judgement of himself? Or were they artworks in themselves?

A tread on the doorstep made him jump.

Don.

He stood there looking in, looking at Hal, at the pictures spread all over the floor. He said nothing, breathing hard.

Hal cowered guiltily. What was he *doing*? What had come over him?

Still not speaking, Don came further in. Carefully he skirted round the easel. He picked up the Stanley knife from the table and put it down again. He stood close to Hal, looking at the three words gashed in red.

'I'm—' Hal tried.

Don's chin jutted. 'See? See? You know now. You know what I really am. Rubbish. Useless. Kuh-c-crap. Can't do anything, can't get anything right. Good idea of yours to trash the place. Go on – what are you waiting for? Chuck it out, chuck everything out.' He gestured towards the pictures on the floor. 'Break them up, smash them, use them for firewood. Yes, let's have a fire! Burn the lot. All this useless old tat. All this detritus. Better burned.'

He lunged towards Hal. Thinking he was going to hit or grab him, Hal sprawled to one side. But Don was aiming at the boards still on the shelf. In a fury he grabbed at them and hauled. He snatched a green pastel from the table-top and scrawled TAT and JUNK on another of the pictures, a delicate seascape, in strokes so fierce that the pastel snapped in two. Then he chucked the pieces aside and began to pull at a big, heavy painting swathed in bubble-wrap.

'Don, stop!' Hal shouted, trying to push it back. 'Stop it! Don't!'

If Don heard, he took no notice at all. Hal clutched his arm, but Don flung his elbow back and threw him off-balance. While he lurched to his feet, Don picked up the Stanley knife and began hacking and tearing at the bubble-wrap, careless of the painting inside.

'This one! This can go first,' he muttered.

'Wait! Stop!' Hal pleaded. 'Let me see.'

It may not have been a good idea to position himself between the sharp blade and the painting, but that's what he'd done, with no time to think. For an instant he saw Don's face, very close, contorted in rage and sorrow, and the Stanley knife gripped tight in his raised hand. Everything went blurry; next moment he heard the knife drop to the floor and clatter on the boards. Neither of them picked it up. Don sat down slowly on the sofa. He lifted both hands to his face, pressing fists into his eyes.

'I didn't mean – my God, Hal! – I didn't mean – I could have—'

Hal was trembling, but found himself saying calmly, 'It's all right. You didn't! It's OK, honest.'

He glanced down, saw the knife lying on the floor, and surreptitiously covered it with his foot.

'But I nearly – could have—' Don wailed. 'As if I haven't done enough damage already!'

'What is it?' Hal asked, to divert him. 'This painting?'

'Heap of old tat. Completely worthless. Waste of paint.'

Don poked at the shredded bubble-wrap with his foot,

then bent down to pull it aside. Hal helped. They both looked at the painting underneath.

Night sky. Stars. Moon, a great curve of it filling a third of the picture, so close that Hal saw craters and ridges and folds in the rock. He felt dizzied by its perspective, as if he were in a spacecraft approaching the lunar surface. Neil Armstrong and Buzz Aldrin must have had a view like this.

There were maybe three or four paintings in the world that Hal could put a name to, and he was gazing at one of them. *Moony*. By Don Inchbold. 1969. Private Collection. Last seen by Hal on the Modern Painters website.

'Is this it? *Moony*? The actual painting?'

'For what it's – nnng – worth,' Don said, subdued now.

'But Aunt Jude told me it was stolen!'

'It was. *I* stole it.'

'What,' Hal mocked, 'stole it from yourself?'

'That's right!' Don was defiant. 'I hid it. Sold it, then changed my mind. Gave the money back. Pretended it was stolen. I didn't want anyone to see it any more.'

'So now you want to slash it to bits? How could you *do* that? Your most famous painting?'

'I don't want it. It's no use to me. You have it, if you like it. And I won't be coming here any more.' Don scuffed his plimsoll on the sandy floorboards.

'Not coming here? Why not?'

'She's chucked me out, Hal. Doesn't want me around. I don't blame her.'

'Aunt Jude? Why?'

'Mucked everything up, didn't I?' Don wiped his nose on the sleeve of the baggy knitted cardigan he was wearing; Hal saw his eyes shiny with tears.

'But – I don't get it. What's happened?'

Don shook his head. 'I can't tell you. We had a blazing row. Ask her. She'll tell you what a – k – useless old fool I am. Waste of space. Nothing but trouble. Sorry – nng – sorry, Hal.'

'Look.' Hal was terrified that Don was actually going to collapse into sobs – *then* what would he do? 'She can't have meant it.'

'She always means what she says. Says what she means,' Don said, his voice wavering.

'No, but she wouldn't, like, really chuck you out – she just wouldn't.' Hal looked around hopelessly for something to make Don feel better; his eye lighted on the kettle. 'Shall I get us a drink or something? Coffee?'

'No. No thanks.' Don bent down, took off one of his plimsolls, tipped small stones out of it, and put it back on; then he stood. 'God, what a mess this place is. Should have had a good sort-out, months ago. You ought to get home,' he told Hal, standing up, straightening, becoming the adult again. 'She's expecting you. Have you – nngg – checked your mobile?'

Remembering that he'd turned it off, Hal delved into his pocket. As soon as he'd entered his code, the symbol for Voicemail came up – two messages.

The first from Mum: 'Hal, call me, please. Soon as you can.'

And the second from Aunt Jude: 'Hal, where are you? Ring me as soon as you get this. Are you on your way back? I'll come and fetch you if not. And leave your phone *on*, this time.'

What was the fuss about? It seemed to have happened a long time ago – the confrontation with Wesley, the call to Mum, the stomping off. He wished he could forget it, wipe the whole Wesley thing from his mind. Wesley wasn't his dad. So what? A week ago he'd never even heard of Wesley. This weird scene with Don made it all seem slightly unreal.

He didn't want to be fetched. Didn't want to go back yet, either. There were more important things going on here.

'I'll stay and—' he began, then realised he was speaking to an empty hut. Don had gone.

Standing on the doorstep, Hal gazed in all directions. He saw a few dog-walkers down on the beach, someone flying a kite, a family playing volleyball. No sign of Don. He hadn't gone down for a swim, then – his yellow oilskin would have been conspicuous, left on the beach. Wasn't walking along the coast path, either.

Hal's first thought was that he was out of his depth, here. Didn't know what Don might do. Best to ring Aunt Jude and get her to come down and take charge.

But maybe Don had only gone for a pee, in the bushes behind the hut. Hal knew that Don often did that rather than walk along to the public loos, some way back in the promenade car park.

Deciding to straighten things up a bit while he waited, Hal went back to the chaos of paintings and wrappings all over the floor. *Moony* lay there, compelling him to gaze at it, pulling him towards the moon's cratered surface.

What now? He couldn't leave it there, visible to anyone who happened to glance through the door. He cleared away the tatters of bubble-wrap, the spawn-like shreds of it, and found an old Tesco bag for rubbish. He swathed the painting in corrugated card, folding and patching, securing it with parcel-tape.

Next, the boards Don had scrawled over. Hal thought he'd better get them out of sight, or Don might start again, defacing more of his work. These were small enough to fit into a large plastic bag, which Hal stowed on the lower shelf. Then he replaced all the rest, all the sketches and paintings he and Don between them had hauled out.

He began on the table-top, tidying as best he could. He threw away the cigarette packet and the pencil sharpenings, stood the paintbrushes in a jar and the pencils in a mug, put all the newspaper clippings and postcards in one heap. A kitchen broom was lying behind the sofa; Hal swept the floor, swept out the sand that had been trodden or blown in to gather in corners and in the cracks between the floorboards. He even took the rug outside and gave it a shaking. He washed the mugs in cold water from the big plastic bottle Don used for topping-up, then filled the kettle, ready to make a hot drink when Don came back.

He felt quite proud of all this sorting and tidying. Mum would have been astonished.

But still no Don.

Looking out of the door, Hal saw Czeszka wandering along the tideline, trailing a piece of orange netting in one hand. He was about to go back in and pretend not to have seen her when she looked up and waved.

How determined she was! He'd cleared off and left her, yesterday, but she seemed to hold no grudge. Apparently she'd decided they were friends, and nothing he did could shake her in that. She hurried up, trailing the netting; she smiled her wide smile.

'Is your grandfather? This artist man?'

'No!' Hal moved aside, letting her see in. 'He's not my grandfather. He's – a friend.'

'He is artist, much famous. Gregor tells me,' Czeszka said solemnly.

'Yes, but—' Hal couldn't begin to explain the gulf between Don's reputation and the shambling, tearful figure who'd been sitting here on the sofa. 'He's not here now. And he doesn't like people calling him famous. He's a bit moody.'

'Moody?'

'Up and down.' Hal made a wave-like motion with his hand.

'Ah. And the other man. Your father. Where is he?'

Hal shook his head, looked down at the ground. 'He's not my father. I got it all wrong.'

Czeszka frowned. 'Not? But how you don't know? Family is so much important. You have family here, yes?'

'Sort of.' He wasn't going to start explaining. 'Let's go and see what the tide's brought in.'

He wanted to shove everything out of his mind again, to run down over the stones, to feel the wind tugging at his hair and salting his face. He threw a clump of seaweed at Czeszka and got a damp faceful in return. He picked up a bit of driftwood and thwacked at the flies that gathered on the drying weed, until the rotting wood split and crumbled into pieces.

Below the high-tide mark, the sand stretched smooth and unblemished, asking to be written on. With a splinter of wood, he scored letters into the sand.

USELESS
RUBBISH
CRAP

Czeszka stood back to read each word aloud. She looked at him in puzzlement.

'What is this? Rude words. Angry words. Why are you so much angry, Hal?'

He said nothing, felt his mouth doing its strange twist.

'Who make you angry?' Czeszka repeated.

'Everyone. No one. Myself.' Hal was still holding the sharp wood fragment. He began making a shallow, twisting pattern in the sand.

Czeszka marched up to USELESS and swept her foot back and forth, obliterating the letters. Faster and faster she stamped. It became a dance, her feet scraping, stamping, skipping. Hal couldn't help laughing, watching her; then she pulled him in, and he began to stamp and scrape too. Soon nothing was left but a welter of footprints.

'Now, I start again.' She picked up the stick Hal had dropped, and moved to fresh sand.

HAL, she wrote. NICE FUNNY FREND.

Then she signed CZESZKA, and drew a flourish underneath.

'Better. Yes?'

Hal nodded, though he couldn't see that it made any difference at all. They were only words. They'd be washed away by the next tide, whether they were good or bad, true or false. And what on earth made her think he was nice and funny? He didn't feel nice. He only felt—

His mobile jingled in his pocket. Aunt Jude. Damn! He should have kept it turned off, but now she'd know she wasn't getting Voicemail. Reluctantly, he accepted the call. 'Yeah.'

'Hal, it's me. Where are you? Didn't you get my message?

Has your mum rung you back? Are you on your way home?
Or with Don? Are you on your own?'

Firing such a barrage of questions, she couldn't expect
answers to all of them. Hal limited himself to the most
convenient.

'Uh. At the beach. Near the hut. He was here. Now he's
gone.'

'Don't go away,' Aunt Jude instructed him. 'Stay where
you are. I'm coming down.'

18
DAMAGE

Hal and Czeszka were sitting on the hut's deck, feet on the steps. Czeszka sat hunched, chin and nose tucked inside her zipped front, hood pulled down, so all that could be seen of her was her eyes; Hal's hands were balled up inside his sleeves. It was too cold to sit doing nothing. He was about to go inside, and in any case he didn't see why Czeszka was hanging around; he hadn't asked her to. Then he saw Aunt Jude hurrying along the row of huts, head bent, red scarf flying out.

'Here she is,' he told Czeszka. 'My aunt.'

Aunt Jude looked disconcerted to find someone else with Hal. 'Oh. I don't think we've met, have we?'

'I am Czeszka. Hal's friend,' Czeszka said importantly.

'Chesska?'

'Czeszka. Franczeszka. Full of zs,' Hal explained.

'Oh! Well, hello, Czeszka,' said Aunt Jude, in a *no-one's-told-me-about-this* sort of way; then she turned to Hal. 'Have you seen him? Don? The hut door's open, so I suppose he must be around.'

'I unlocked it, though. He leaves the key under that stone.' Hal showed her where. 'It's stupid, with his paintings in here, the moon one and everything. Anyone could get in here and nick them.'

'What did you say?' Aunt Jude said sharply. 'The moon?'

'Yeah, the *Moony* painting, the famous one. It's on the shelf there.'

'*What?* It can't be! It went missing years ago. I've never even seen it. He must have done a copy.'

'I'm sure it's the one.' But Hal felt less certain now. 'At least, he didn't *say* it was a copy. He just said it was a heap of old tat.'

'Let me see.' Aunt Jude was inside now, looking at the easel and the table, bending down to the shelves. 'What an awful mess! I can't think how he works in such chaos.'

Huh! She should have seen it *before*.

Carefully, Hal manoeuvred out the heavy painting and tore at the parcel-tape he'd taken such care with. Getting it all stuck round his hands, he reached for the Stanley knife and sliced with that instead. At last the painting lay there, revealed. Aunt Jude moved round to study it from the best angle.

'Well, I don't know. I'm no expert. Can't tell if it's a copy or not.'

'Is amazing! Beautiful!' Czeszka said, bending close. 'Amanda tell me about this. She show me and Gregor in a book. Now I see it real, and is better. She would much like for the gallery, I think.'

Hal explained, 'Czeszka's brother works at that new lifeboat centre. Amanda's the person who came here looking for Don that time.'

Aunt Jude nodded. 'I can't believe Don would ever do a copy of something he'd sold – he'd never do the same thing twice. But fancy him keeping it here like this! How did you know, Hal?'

'He showed me, but then he – uh—'

Aunt Jude jumped into the pause. 'He what?'

'He – started going at it with the knife.'

'No!' Her hand flew to her mouth. 'While you were here? He didn't, though? Didn't do any damage?'

Hal shook his head.

'When was this? How long ago?'

Hal thought. 'Hour ago? Maybe less?'

'And it was that knife he had, that one there? He hasn't got a knife with him now?'

'Don't think so.' Hal began covering up the *Moony* picture again.

'I'm going to look for him.' Aunt Jude was already moving towards the door. 'D'you want to come with me, Hal, or stay here with, er, Czeszka?'

She must have thought better of throwing Don out, forgotten the blazing row Don said they'd had. She wanted him back after all.

'I'll come,' Hal said, picking up urgency from her tone.

Aunt Jude jingled the keys in her pocket. 'We'll take the car. Czeszka, can I give you a lift home?'

'Thank you, no. I promise help Gregor.'

Hal locked up, putting the key back under its stone. They walked back to Aunt Jude's Focus, parked as near as she could get it to the beach huts, and Czeszka set off towards the lifeboat-house.

'You didn't tell me you'd made a friend.' Aunt Jude

started the engine, and looked over her shoulder before reversing.

'Oh, I've met her a couple of times. She hangs out at the beach.'

'Your mum phoned. She told me you've been to see Wesley Prince.' Aunt Jude's voice was carefully matter-of-fact.

'Don told me you've had a blazing row,' Hal countered.

'Did he? Oh, dear . . . yes. Put your seatbelt on, Hal.'

'He says you've chucked him out.'

She glanced at him. 'I – I said some awful things. I—' But she stopped there, biting her lip, shaking her head rapidly. It unnerved Hal. She was always so much in control, so sure of herself.

Hal had no idea where they'd start looking, or how being in the car would help, but Aunt Jude turned along the narrow road that ran behind the beach huts, heading away from town. She drove slowly, while Hal scanned the scrubby bushes and trees to the landward side.

'He'll be back. He'll turn up when he feels like it. I might as well go home and cook the lunch, really, but – Hal, this is all my fault!'

'*What* is?

'I got it all wrong. I'm sorry, really sorry. *I* thought Wesley Prince was your father. It was my mistake, Hal. I started all this.'

'He isn't,' Hal said, as if the idea were stupid.

'No, I know now. Tina rang me straight after she'd spoken to you. She didn't know anything about Wesley being here, and I – like a fool – I just assumed. I'd known about Tina and Wesley – they were going out together when I was still here. Then I left for Portugal, and she went off to Manchester. When she told her parents she was pregnant, there was a big row, and she cut herself off from all of us. So I didn't even know, till the funeral, that your father's black. When I saw you, I just took it for granted that Wesley was your father.'

Hal tugged at his seatbelt. 'But you told Don!'

'I know, and I shouldn't have. And he had no reason to doubt it. That's why it was so unfair of me to—'

They'd arrived at a public parking place, a gravelly area with low cliffs below. Aunt Jude pulled in, got out of the car and scanned the shore in both directions.

'To what?' Hal prompted, since she'd left her sentence unfinished. 'Unfair to do what?'

'I lost my temper – really lost it. Told him to get out of the house. Told him he was an interfering old fool, for stirring things up, encouraging you to find Wesley. Said I didn't want him cluttering up my life anymore. I said . . . awful, horrible things, Hal. And now look!'

'So – that's all because of me, too?' Hal said. 'The row? Because of me going after Wesley?'

'No, you mustn't blame yourself. I was out of order, the way I ranted. I ought to know he wouldn't put up with that. Why should he?'

For the second time, Hal found himself trying to re-assure an adult. 'He'll be back. He won't have gone far. I'd have found Wesley anyway, whether Don said or not.'

'I know – all because I've been stupid. I shouldn't have taken it out on him. Perhaps he's back at the hut by now? Or at home? We'll drive along a bit farther, then go back. He might have set off on one of his long walks. How did he seem?'

'Oh, you know. A bit, like, flaky. Then he seemed to

cheer up, and next minute he was gone.' He couldn't tell Aunt Jude that Don had been *crying*. That had shocked Hal more than he liked to think.

What he'd said was enough to scare Aunt Jude into silence as they drove back the way they'd come. Any minute now, Hal thought, they'd meet Don shambling along the road, and he'd exchange a few insults with Aunt Jude, and everything would be back to normal.

Aunt Jude parked in the same place as before, on the sandy slip-road that led down towards the huts. Hal ran ahead, but could already see that the hut door was closed. He pressed his nose against the glass. Inside, everything was just as they'd left it.

Hal waited for Aunt Jude to catch up.

'Still not here?' Her face sagged with disappointment.

'Hasn't he got a mobile? Couldn't you leave him a voice-mail?'

'No,' said Aunt Jude, with an effort at smiling. 'He's far too pig-headed to have anything so useful. I bought him one for Christmas and he gave it to someone he met on the beach. Can you believe it?'

'Yeah, I can.'

'He'll be back,' Aunt Jude said resolutely. 'He'll turn up.'

The more she kept saying that, the more Hal saw how worried she was. How she was only trying to convince herself, to sound like nothing was really wrong. What did she think had happened? Might Don just keep on going, whichever direction he'd taken? Hitch a lift to Portsmouth and get on a boat for France? Simply walk out of their lives?

'He doesn't usually carry money on him, apart from a

bit of change,' Aunt Jude said, as if reading Hal's thoughts. 'No bank card or anything like that. He can't go far, only on his own two feet.'

'What about the police, then? Should you call them?'

Aunt Jude looked startled. 'Police? No, no. What would I say? A man's gone for a walk? They'd tell me to get a grip.'

'P'raps he's back at home now.'

'Yes.' Aunt Jude seized on this; she took out her phone, pressed keys and waited, the eagerness on her face fading to despondency. 'No answer. But he's quite likely not to pick up even if he's there, if he's got himself in a state.'

'Why don't you drive back and see?' Hal suggested. 'I'll wait here.'

'But I don't like to – oh well, all right. I'll come straight back if he's not there. Your mobile's on?'

She hurried to the car. Hal waited in the hut, getting cold all over again. An electric heater stood in one corner and he considered plugging it in, but was too restless to stay. He wanted to produce Don like a prize for Aunt Jude when she returned. He wanted to get something right.

Outside, he gazed along the length of the beach. They might have missed something, from the car; Don might be meandering along the shore. His eyes strained; he willed Don to appear.

A splash of brightness leapt out at him. Something yellow, dumped on the pebbles.

Don's oilskin! He must be there, swimming, probably, cold though it was. Joyfully, Hal bounded over, skidding on the stones. The tide was coming in now, washing over the words Czeszka had inscribed.

Hal could already picture Aunt Jude's relief, and hear the volley of insults she'd fire at Don.

He gazed out at the sea. Cold, grey and uninviting it looked; but then, Don was used to it. He was as mad as those people Hal had seen on TV, breaking ice to swim on Christmas Day. Hal narrowed his eyes, searching for Don's bobbing head.

Immediately he found it – a small dark blob, far out. But he had the feeling that something was wrong. Don, if it was Don, didn't appear to be swimming, just floating, or treading water. Hal held up a hand and peered again. Maybe his eyes were playing tricks: maybe it wasn't Don at all, but a floating buoy, or a stray football, bobbing, sometimes hidden in the hollow of the waves. But if that wasn't Don, then where? Was this what Aunt Jude feared – that he might simply strike out into the vastness, never come back?

Then Hal saw the movement of a hand above the surface – not swimming, not waving. The feeblest gesture, it looked, of someone barely alive.

Hal hesitated. There was no one he could shout to for help; the nearest people were small specks, too far away to hear him yell.

Making up his mind, he kicked off his trainers and ran down the sand and into the breakers.

'Don! I'm coming!' he shouted, though he couldn't even see Don now, and his words were snatched away and carried inland.

The coldness repelled him; his jeans clammed against his legs, his toes winced at the sharpness of pebbles. He made himself wade farther in, gasping as the chill water rose up his body in a series of fresh shocks, his clothes sagging and clinging. Impossibly, aggressively cold, it seemed – clamping him, numbing him. He hadn't swum in the sea for ages, and didn't want to now, but what was the choice? Stand on the beach and watch Don drown? Tell Aunt Jude he'd been too much of a wimp to do anything about it?

The sand shelved under his feet. He launched himself, and felt the icy slap in his face, the tangy splutter of salt in his mouth. He pushed himself into a flailing crawl. What an encumbrance his clothes were, heavy and sogged! But it would take too long to stop and peel them off. Worse, he couldn't see Don, had lost sight of that small bobbing head, that tiny marker. All he could see was the sway and tilt of the waves. He felt himself lifted and carried on an inrush, losing the small progress he'd made. He swallowed water, coughed, spluttered. The sea was huge: around him, below him. Almost, even, above him. It was overwhelming. He was a strong swimmer, he'd have said, but that was in the tameness of the public pool. This vast, heaving sea might have been made of a different element.

How far out was he? How far could he go? He paused to tread water and look back at the shore. Yes, it was still reachable. The tide was coming in; it wouldn't fight him. The fight was now, pushing out against the current, caught off-stroke every time by the wash and slap and thrust.

'Don!' he tried shouting. 'Don!' His throat was parched with salt, his eyes stinging with it. He succeeded only in losing his rhythm and getting a fresh mouthful as his head went under.

What would it be like to drown? To let yourself be taken? The breathing and sighing of the waves, moon-pulled, could get into your head, mesmerising. If you stopped thinking about the cold you could almost be soothed by it. You could forget to swim, forget to breathe, forget that land was where you belonged. Give yourself up. And then . . . eventually, you'd be washed up on the shore, limp as a starfish.

Is that what Don was doing? Such a strange mood he'd been in.

'Don!' Hal yelled, in panic.

Was someone answering, or had he imagined it? A voice, a high note above the wind, or just the cry of a gull? He stopped swimming, raised his head and looked first out to sea, then back at the shore.

'Hal! Hal!' Aunt Jude stood on the beach, waving frantically. And close by, waist-deep in the water, pointing, was – Don.

What? What was going on? Hal stared, went under, clawed to the surface, stared again.

Don. Not an illusion. Safe. Alive.

'Hal!' Aunt Jude shouted again. 'Come back!'

Hal waved to show he'd heard. Immediately, Don plunged in, and struck out in a powerful crawl, heading towards him.

How stupid to drown *now* . . .

So tired he was, so mind-numbingly cold, so hampered by the weight of his clothes – how much energy did he have left? He'd changed to breaststroke, less demanding of effort, but he felt no more effective than a bundle of rags drifting with the tide.

Then Don was there, swift and sure as Hal was feeble, taking his arm in a firm grip. 'I've got you!'

'I'm OK!' Hal spluttered, though he wasn't. He didn't want the embarrassment of being towed to safety by Don, instead of the other way round. All the same, Don kept close by, guiding, glancing, as they turned for the shore.

At last, Hal's feet met the yielding softness of sand, and he was stumbling upright, water streaming from clothes and hair. He staggered and overbalanced; his legs were like rubber. This was how Channel swimmers must feel when they reached the coast of France. The wind and the air were cold on his skin.

Aunt Jude rushed up to embrace him, soaked as he was. 'Hal! Thank God! What were you *doing*?'

19
SANDFATHER

'Trying to save *me*?' Don was baffled. 'But I was only having my dip, same as usual. A walk and a swim. Nothing I needed rescuing from.'

They were picking their way back to the hut, Hal in bare feet, dangling his trainers by their laces. Aunt Jude clung to his arm. She'd insisted on wrapping him in Don's oil-skin coat, while Don only had a jersey slung round his shoulders. They were all talking at once:

'But what made you—'

'I just thought—'

'All my stupid fault—'

'You must be *frozen*—'

'No, I'm OK, honest—'

Now that they were together and safe, Aunt Jude was even more agitated than before. 'Hal, you could have been swept out to sea – got cramp or hypothermia – got yourself exhausted, searching – oh, I can't bear to think about it! Plunging in with all your clothes on! You brave, silly boy!' She rounded on Don. 'Oh, what a pig's ear we've made of things, the two of us! What a pair of idiots – me especially!'

Before they'd got as far as the hut, it began to seem funny. Larky. They went in, and Don switched on the electric fire, which soon gave out a warming glow. Aunt Jude laid the oilskin out to dry, and made Hal take off his wet clothes and wrap himself in the blanket from the sofa. Don got dressed, and rubbed his hair on a piece of old sacking that had been used to wrap one of the pictures. While Aunt Jude made hot drinks, Don brought out a packet of biscuits that Hal hadn't found in his tidying. It felt like an absurd picnic. Here they were, together, smiling and laughing, the three of them. No one lost, no one drowned. Hal wriggled his toes in the warmth of the fire's glow.

'What am I going to tell your mum?' Aunt Jude kept saying.

'Just tell her Hal fancied a swim.' Don put a whole biscuit in his mouth and crunched it noisily.

Aunt Jude touched his arm. 'You'll come home now, Don, won't you? Please? After all this, I want us to be together today.'

Don nodded. 'Yes. The three of us.'

Time was behaving strangely. Back at the house, Aunt Jude made Hal have a hot bath. In spite of all that had happened, it was still only two o'clock. The Sunday lunch Aunt Jude had mentioned hadn't yet got as far as the oven, so Don took over the cooking while Hal spoke to

Mum on the phone – glossing over his failed attempt at life-saving. While the joint of pork was roasting, Hal raked up drifts of leaves in the garden, and Aunt Jude did some pruning and tidying, piling up twigs and clippings for a bonfire.

'Guy Fawkes' night, soon,' Don said, coming out to see how they were doing.

Hal thought of Hallowe'en, and of Firework Night – last year Osman's family had had a fireworks party and barbecue, and maybe they'd do it again. And Christmas wasn't far off. He'd be back home by then, not with Aunt Jude and Don any more. Not by the sea, either. He didn't want to think about that. Today it seemed impossible to think of being anywhere but here.

They were all treating each other carefully and kindly.

In the garden, Aunt Jude apologised again for misleading Hal about Wesley; he shrugged it off, as if it were some trivial thing. He'd made an idiot of himself, and was fatherless all over again, but his brain refused to go there, not yet. His mind, as well as his body, was exhausted. He remembered times when he'd hurt himself, banged into something hard, slammed his hip or his shin; how it took a few beats for the pain to register, though he knew it was coming. And when it did, for that moment it was as much as he knew how to bear.

Don came out from the cooking with a pair of kitchen scissors, looking for thyme. When he'd cut a few sprigs he came over to Hal, cleared his throat, and said, 'What you did, er, trying to – you know – save me.'

'Yeah,' said Hal, not looking at him. 'It was stupid.'

'Nng. I never said thank you. It – k – means a lot to me.'

Hal shook his head. 'Don't worry about it.' He continued trundling the green wheelie-bin towards the side of the house, and the awkward exchange was over.

The light faded early, and with the dusk came a feeling of anticipation, of winter and coldness, and long nights. They ate their late dinner at the kitchen table. Don lit candles: 'To mark the coming of darkness.' He'd strewn the table with evergreen leaves and red-orange berries, rescued from the pruning, and the black berry-like fruits of ivy. And he'd added special touches to the meal: tangy apple sauce, and mulled wine, and plum crumble to follow. It felt like a celebration; of life, of being together.

Don poured hot wine for himself and Aunt Jude, and gave Hal some to taste. Hal didn't like it much, but he needed it for when Don raised his glass, looked at Aunt Jude and then at Hal, and said, 'To us. To the three of us.'

They clinked their glasses together and drank, and Hal looked at the two faces in the candlelight and saw what a pair they were, Aunt Jude and Don, in their strange way. No matter how much they complained, no matter how many insults they threw at each other: they belonged together.

It was later, when the charmed circle of the table was broken, when the washing-up was done and everything cleared away, and Aunt Jude and Don were in the front room with the Sunday papers and the last of the wine and a music CD, that reality began to creep back.

He'd failed. He'd achieved nothing. All his wanting, all his brief certainty, all his searching and hoping – it added up to nothing. He was back where he'd been before. Mum would come down, and be sorry, and be all over him, but still she'd fob him off. Don might talk of 'the three of us', but really he meant himself and Aunt Jude. They'd be glad to get rid of him, to have the place to themselves. He was just a temporary nuisance. He'd soon be back at school, with his On Report cards, and his Anger Management, whatever that turned out to mean.

Upstairs in his room, he took out the bag of marbles from his rucksack. An age ago, it seemed, he'd produced them in triumph for Wesley, as proof. Now he thought of throwing them away, taking them down to the dustbin this minute. Mum would tell him not to waste them, to give them to a charity shop. Whatever.

He reached into the bag and took one out.

The white one, the swirly white one. It sat in the palm of his hand like a small moon.

The phone rang; he heard Aunt Jude answer. He listened intently in case it was Mum, but it didn't seem to be, and Aunt Jude was speaking too quietly for him to pick out what she was saying. Then footsteps came up the stairs, and she looked in at his door.

'Hal? It's Wesley on the phone. He'd like to speak to you. You don't have to if you'd rather not. He said that.'

Hal's first reaction was to shake his head and shrug, but curiosity was too strong. He slipped the moon-marble back into its bag and ran down to the phone.

'Hi.' He didn't know how to speak to Wesley.

'Hi, Hal,' said Wesley's deep voice. 'I hope you don't mind me phoning. I was a bit worried after you rushed off. And I wanted to ask about Tina, but your aunt says she's out of hospital now and doing well.'

'Uh. Yeah.'

'So you're here till the weekend? There's lots going on at the leisure centre – five-a-side football – coaching – weights

– all sorts. You've got a friend staying down here, your aunt says – it'd be great to have you along, both of you, if you're at a loose end.'

'Uh. OK. I might.'

'Hope to see you, then, Hal.'

'Thanks. See you.' Hal rang off.

'All right?' said Aunt Jude, coming slowly down the stairs.

'All right. I'm going to bed now.'

The Sandfather came back to him, in a dream. This time, Hal was in the sea, swimming, struggling to get back to shore. The more he kicked and fought, the bigger the waves heaved, the farther the beach retreated. And the sandman stood there upright, looking with his marble eyes. Looking out to sea, looking for Hal – disappointed in him, in his feeble efforts.

A wind was rising. Flurries of sand whipped along the beach like a dust storm. Sand streamed like veils from the Sandfather's head, from his shoulders, his arms, his legs. He couldn't stand up to this. When Hal tried to shout, his mouth filled with salt water. Choking, he went under.

He clawed for the surface, broke clear, breathed again. His eyes were stinging as he gazed towards the shore. A large wave broke, and now, where the Sandfather had stood, there was nothing but washed, shining sand.

Hal woke up with tears streaming down his cheeks and into his ears. He didn't try to stop them.

20
NOT

It was still half-term week, but Hal felt like someone recovering from an illness: venturing outside, beginning to do normal things, but constantly pulled into himself, to the ache there.

Gently, Aunt Jude guided him back to his school-work, not yet finished. He did it mechanically, with only the surface part of his mind. The tocking clock in the dining room had somehow become part of the sea's rhythm, part of his own heartbeat and the swooshing of blood in his veins.

He was still waiting, always waiting. Waiting for Mum, now. For her to come, and tell him who he was. Where his missing half came from.

On Tuesday he went sailing again, with Luke, Luke's dad and Mike, and Mike's wife Sarah. The day was bright and dazzling, the light sharp.

Reluctantly, Hal told Luke, 'You know what I said about my dad? It's not true. I got it all wrong.'

Luke nodded, as if he already knew. Maybe Aunt Jude had found a way of telling Graham. But Luke didn't tease Hal, as he once would have. He seemed to realise that Hal had been through something painful, and needed time to recover.

As soon as the admission was made, Hal felt better. There was no need to talk about it any more. He could concentrate on the physical demands of sailing; of anticipating the next tack, being in the right place before he was asked, knowing which sheet needed hauling in or letting out. The feeling of riding the waves and the wind was exhilarating: being in control and out of control, both at once.

'Getting your sea-legs, now,' Mike told him. 'You and Luke make a good team.'

Team. And not just for sailing. At least Hal needn't dread the return to school quite as much; he'd got his friend back.

They stayed out longer this time, and sailed in as the light faded to dusk, navigating by the lights on the buoys that marked the harbour entrance. Mike was talking now of an idea for spring half-term, hiring the yacht again and taking it all the way across to St Malo in Brittany, stopping off at one of the Channel Islands. Luke and Hal and Graham could come, as crew, sleeping on board in the tiny cabins.

'We should get Oz to come, as well,' said Luke. 'He's never sailed.'

'More the merrier,' Mike said easily.

Getting the boat ready for mooring – sails down, fenders

out, lines cleated and coiled fore and aft – Hal felt like an old hand. He'd be able to show Oz a thing or two when he came on board knowing nothing.

Don was painting again. Aunt Jude said she could tell, because he wasn't quite all there. He turned up at meal-times, same as usual, but he was distracted, caught up in the vision in his mind. When Hal asked him *what* he was painting, Don wouldn't say. 'If it's any good, I'll show you. Probably turn out to be rubbish.' But Hal could tell he didn't really believe that. There was a new energy about him, an eagerness.

On Tuesday evening, after they'd eaten and cleared up, he told them that he'd made a decision.

'About *Moony.* I've offered it to the Lifeboat Gallery, on loan. May as well brush the cobwebs off, let it see the light of day. It'll get that harpy off my back, that Amanda whatsaname.'

Aunt Jude looked staggered.

'Oh, Don! That's a great idea. They'll be delighted, the gallery people. It'll give them a terrific boost. Great for publicity.'

Publicity wasn't Don's favourite word. 'Well. Provided no one comes bothering me, they can have it for however long they want.'

'We'll go, on Saturday,' Aunt Jude announced. 'To the launch party. We'll all go. I'll ask Tina as well, if it's not too much for her. We'll all be so proud of you. Yes, we *will*

– don't make such a grumpy face, Don! Take a bit of credit for once.'

Mum was coming down on Thursday, in Claire's car. Claire would stay for lunch, then drive back; Mum was to sleep in her old room, in her old bed, with Hal downstairs on the sofa. Then, on Sunday, Aunt Jude would drive Mum and Hal home, and that would be it. His stay at Ryton would be over. The days were running out, and already he felt the ache of leaving. It was amazing how quickly being here had come to seem normal; how Aunt Jude and Don seemed like family he'd known for years and years.

After dinner, Don disappeared. Hal thought he'd gone back to his flat, or down to the hut to paint, but then he burst in while Hal and Aunt Jude were watching TV.

'Come on out, you two! You can't – nng – sit here glued to that tosh. Put your coats on. Come outside.'

He led them out to the garden. It was a clear, starry night. They all stood looking up. More and more stars pricked through the darkness. As his eyes adjusted, Hal felt dizzied, as if he might fall right off the Earth and find himself swimming through stars. And there was a new moon, the merest sliver, like a silver nail-clipping. How fantastic! How brilliant, how dazzling, how mind-boggling the night was, and he'd been sitting indoors quite unaware.

'D'you know your way around?' Don asked him.

'Well, I know the Plough.' Hal pointed. 'There it is. And Orion. That's easy.'

But – he looked around, getting a crick in his neck from gazing – the Orion constellation was nowhere to be seen.

'He'll be down on the horizon – round in the west by early morning,' said Don. 'See Cassiopeia, though, the big

W? And Ursa Minor, the Little Bear, like the Plough only smaller? And look – there's too much light everywhere, these days, but you can just get an idea of the Milky Way – see where the stars are thickest – like a long scarf trailing across the sky?'

They looked and looked. Aunt Jude got cold and went indoors; Hal and Don stayed outside until Hal too was chilled and giddied, ready to fall asleep on his feet.

'Didn't know you knew so much,' Hal said, gratefully entering the warmth of the kitchen.

'Hardly anything at all, when you think how much there *is* to know. If you're interested, we ought to get hold of a – k! – telescope. Go down to the beach one clear night.'

'But there aren't many nights left. This time next week I'll be at home.'

'Mmnng. And your grandfather'll be here. All change,' Don said gloomily.

Hal hadn't thought about that. Where would that leave Don, when the grandfather was back? Aunt Jude would move into her own flat, then. Maybe Don would go and live in the beach hut.

On Thursday, Hal went with Luke to the leisure centre, for football coaching. Wesley was heading for the pool; he waved and smiled and said, 'Catch you later.'

'Is that him?' Luke asked; Hal nodded, and that was all that was said.

Hal enjoyed the football: mind and body working together, using old skills and building new ones, with a coach and a young player from Southampton United. Both Hal and Luke came in for praise and encouragement, and finished the session feeling good, keen for more.

They paused to look at the Circus Skills group in the

gym, which Hal would quite like to have tried. People were juggling, walking on stilts, attempting to cross a low wire. To his surprise Hal saw Czeszka, high on stilts and walking quite effectively. He pointed her out to Luke, who immediately started on about her being Hal's girlfriend.

'Duh! Don't be stupid!' Hal retorted. 'I hardly know her. Seen her around, that's all.'

But the more fiercely he denied it, the more Luke joked and insinuated. Hal gave up.

Next day was *The* Day. The day Mum was arriving, with Claire. The day she'd tell him. The day he'd find out who his father was.

From the moment Hal woke up, he was alert and excited. Anxious, too. Oddly, now that the finding-out was so close, he felt that maybe he didn't *want* to know. If it wasn't Wesley, who else could be as good? How could some complete stranger take over, fill the gap?

It was too *big* to be filled. Maybe that was the problem. And the stranger, whoever he was, couldn't be more than a distant speck, as far away and as small as one of the stars in the Milky Way.

They arrived at twelve, in Claire's car. Mum greeted Hal as if they'd been separated for many months. In jeans and bright T-shirt, she looked much more her normal self than when he'd seen her in hospital. Claire left soon after lunch, with strict instructions to Mum not to tire herself, and to phone as soon as she got home on Sunday.

They stood in the road while the car turned the corner and out of sight, Claire waving till the last moment. Wanting Mum to himself, Hal was glad she'd gone.

Mum knew what he was waiting for.

'I think I'll unpack my things now,' she said. 'Come and give me a hand, Hal?'

Aunt Jude had stripped and changed the bed for Mum, and put out a clean towel. Hal's few clothes hadn't been back on their hangers since Mum had put them there, and had now been tidied and folded by Aunt Jude. Mum hung her trousers, tops and jacket in the wardrobe, and put her nightdress under the pillow.

At first, she seemed to be avoiding the subject that was hanging unspoken in the air. 'How was the sailing?' she asked instead. And: 'I hear you're friends with Luke again? That's good.'

Maybe she'd changed her mind. Maybe she wasn't going to tell him after all.

'Mum,' he prompted. 'You said you'd . . .'

'I know.' She sat on the bed and gestured him to sit beside her; she gave him a big hug. 'Hal, you know I love you more than anything, don't you? More than anyone in the world?'

'Uh.' Hal squirmed; her hair tickled his cheek and he smelled her perfume. He wished she wouldn't talk like that. Even though it was nice to know.

'And I'd never do anything to hurt you. That's why I've never told you before.'

He looked at her sidelong. 'Told me what?'

'What I'm going to tell you now.' She paused. 'I'm sorry, really sorry for all this confusion, about Wesley I mean. I had no idea he was living here again. If I *had* known—'

'Yeah, what?'

'Well! I might have told you that he used to be my boyfriend, but he's definitely not your father. I could have saved you that disappointment. If you could choose yourself a – a dad, you'd probably choose someone like Wesley. I can see that.'

'So why did you have to dump him, then?'

'Oh . . .' Mum smiled, shook her head. 'It wasn't like that. We were just too young. Wesley was lovely, and we had great times together. He was fun, he was kind, he was – well, gorgeous. But I didn't want to tie myself down. Didn't want *him* to, either. We were both going our different ways. We went off to university. Him to Loughborough, me to Manchester.'

'And, what, you met someone else there?'

'Yes. Yes, I did. He, your father, reminded me of Wesley – that's what attracted me, at first. He was black, obviously. Tall, handsome, athletic. Only not as – Hal, he was a few years older than me. He was a mature student. And he was already married.'

Hal took this in. 'You had a thing going with a married man?'

'I did. And I can't say I'm proud of myself for that. But at the time I – I thought I loved him. I thought he loved *me*. Maybe I did, maybe he did, for a while. Six months, it lasted, just about. It ended when I found I was pregnant. When I told him.'

'So – what happened then? Did his wife find out?'

'I don't think so. He was desperate to keep it secret. He was horrified. He – wanted me to have an abortion, Hal. Pleaded with me. Offered to pay.'

'But you didn't?'

Mum gave a sort of sobbing laugh, leaned against him, hugged him again. 'Of *course* I didn't! Here you are – the best thing in my life!'

'So what, then? Did you dump him?'

'I think we dumped each other. It was finished. He didn't want any more to do with me – I was a nuisance, a threat. And I didn't want anything to do with him, if he expected me to get rid of the baby I wanted so much. So that was that. I left Manchester – well, you know that. Never finished my course. And then – then there was the big row with my parents. My father especially.'

'What did he say?'

Mum shifted on the bed, wriggled herself into a more comfortable position. 'Oh – I was a disgrace to the family, I'd thrown away my chances. Look at it from their point of view, Hal. They'd set their hearts on me getting a degree – they'd have been so proud. They'd put a lot of money into helping me through. And now I was throwing it all back in their faces. Giving up.'

'So they chucked you out?'

'No! They didn't chuck me out. That was my decision. I decided to go my own way. I didn't want their support, not if I was such a disappointment.'

Hal was picking at a loose thread on the duvet cover. 'Did they want you to – you know – get rid of me, too?'

'Yes, they did. At the time. They thought I'd made a huge mistake, and I shouldn't let it dictate my future. Maybe I had – made a mistake. But it gave me the best thing in my whole life, so how could I possibly regret it? And I never have. Not for a single millisecond. Truly, Hal.'

'They wanted you to get rid of me,' Hal repeated, thinking *and now I'm in their house*. 'Was it because –

like – were they racist? Because my father was black? Was that why? Is that why I'd never seen them? Is that why you never really told me about them?'

'No!' Mum shook her head vehemently. 'It was nothing to do with that! Is that what you've been thinking? Oh, Hal, I should have explained; I've always known I should, but I didn't know where to start – or where to stop. The fact is, they didn't *know*. I didn't tell them. I didn't want them to have anything to do with you. *Or* with me. I went off on my own. They never saw you – not till this summer. I mean my dad saw you – it was too late for Mum. And by then he'd realised how stupid it's been, this quarrel going on for so many years. How much he's missed.' She rubbed Hal's arm, looked at him closely. 'It's an awful lot to take in, isn't it? Too much, all at once.'

'No, go on,' Hal said quickly. 'I can – you know – think about it all later.' He didn't want to skip over anything, while Mum was in this talkative mood. It might not happen again.

'I mean, he liked Wesley. He really did,' she went on. 'And I suppose – like Aunt Jude – he must think you're Wesley's son. Maybe I should have explained to him, about your real father. But maybe it's too late for that now. You're you, and that's all that matters.'

'But there's something you, uh, still haven't told me. My father's name.'

Mum looked away from him, out of the window.

'No. And I'm not going to.'

'*What?*' He couldn't believe it. 'But you *promised*!'

'Not yet, Hal. And I didn't promise that. When you're older, when you're eighteen, I'll tell you what you want to know – if you still *do* want it. You might not. After all, you know he didn't want you to be born.'

Hal considered this. He wondered what he thought about this man, this father. Who must *be* somewhere, now this minute, and had been, all those years. Surely, surely he couldn't have forgotten that he had a son? Surely he must *wonder,* sometimes?

'Has he got other kids?'

'I don't know. He didn't, then.'

'So I might have half-brothers and sisters. Younger than me, they'd be. And what about—' He thought of Wesley's father, the Jamaican accent and all it carried with it. 'Is he, like, Afro-Caribbean? Or from where? You can tell me that, can't you?'

'Not Jamaican. Barbados. Still Afro-Caribbean.'

Hal tried it. 'Barbados. Bar*ba*dos.' Felt it on his lips and tongue, its energy, its strong syllables, its hissing finish. *Bar-bay-doss.*

He saw a holiday-advert kind of scene: a sweeping curve of beach, palm trees, lush greenery, deep blue sea. And beyond that was music, rhythm. People. Voices. Ways of living, of belonging, of being. One word from his mum, and it was part of him. Part of who he was, waiting to be found.

Maybe that was why he was so drawn to the beach. It was Barbados calling to him through his blood and his genes. And farther back, Africa, the huge continent full of possibilities.

'Cool,' he said.

21
LIFEBOAT

Marborough's was sold. The sale, all the solicitor business Aunt Jude had been so involved with, was completed. A builder's sign went up outside; it was screened off, boards blocking the pavement, with a pedestrian walkway taking up part of the road. Work would begin next week.

Hal, his mum and Aunt Jude looked at it from their seats in the coffee shop opposite.

'It's sad,' said Mum, 'to think it's not going to be there any more, the old shop.'

'I remember your dad walking round all the departments, every day, first thing and last,' Aunt Jude told her. 'All those memories – he'll miss it, I know.'

Mum was only allowed to do very short walks, warned not to tire herself. From the sea-front car park was enough; now a reviving cappuccino for her, double espresso for Aunt Jude, choco-latte and raspberry muffin for Hal.

'If you wanted to do, like, psychology,' Hal asked her, 'how come you're a hairdresser?'

'One thing led to another. When I thought of leaving Manchester and setting up on my own, I couldn't think where to start. No job, no money, no qualifications – I thought I'd be penniless on the streets. But one thing I was sure of – I wasn't going to run home, asking for help.'

Aunt Jude sighed. 'Silly girl. I only wish I'd known. You're every bit as obstinate as your dad! Always have been.'

'So what happened?' Hal asked.

'I only told two of my friends, Jenna and Claire,' Mum said. 'Claire was the one who solved the problem. Her older brother was working in the States for six months, and he had a bedsit near where we live now. Claire asked if I could have it, and he agreed, as long as I paid the bills. So I moved in, and Jacky was next door. She's a single mum too, so she helped me sort out allowances and benefits, and lent me lots of baby stuff. I was clueless, but I had to learn somehow. She was the biggest help.'

'And then?'

'Well, she was just starting up JJ's. It was her dream. Her own salon. She'd been left some money by her grandma, and that gave her the chance to do it. I knew nothing about hairdressing, but she took me on part-time, to help out. I was cleaner, accountant—'

'Runs in the family,' said Aunt Jude.

'—receptionist, general dogsbody. Earned enough to pay the rent, once the six months was up, and we moved into a council flat. Then Jacky said – a joke, at first – why didn't I train as a stylist? So I did a course, one day a week – she helped finance me through that. And soon, I found the thing that really fascinated me – talking to people. And even more important, listening to them. It's quite staggering, the things people tell their hairdresser! And sometimes, you know, I really feel I've helped someone. Given them an idea, helped them solve a problem, or make up their mind about something that bothers them. Sometimes all I've done is listen, but that's enough.'

'Agony aunt,' said Hal.

Mum smiled. 'And I like the work. Accidental hairdresser, that's me.'

'Now, though?' said Aunt Jude. 'You can always find hairdressing work.'

Mum made a *search me* face. 'Maybe. Maybe not. Could be time for a change.'

It made Hal feel weird, all this. His life seemed such a fixed and definite thing, as if it couldn't possibly have been any different. Yet all of it – his actual existence – depended on chance meetings, decisions, mistakes, offers and suggestions. Here he was, though: himself. He felt solid enough.

Still, there was that name, elusive as a wisp of smoke; the name he still didn't know. He tried again to get it from Mum – pleaded, begged, sulked – but she wouldn't budge.

Down at the beach hut, he sought Don's help.

'She still won't tell me who he *is*! His name! She's told me other stuff, but not that. It's well out of order!'

Don was painting, though he wouldn't let Hal see what. He continued, frowning and scowling over his Daler board, while Hal told him what he did know. Then he said nothing for quite a long time.

'So, come on!' Hal demanded. 'She's got to tell me, hasn't she?'

Don considered the matter for a bit longer. Then he said, 'You know what strikes me? You're best off without him. He's a father, but not a dad. And only a father in the strictest biological sense. What else has he done? He's been no use to you, probably never will be. But you've got family, Hal, a family that loves you and wants you and needs you. You've got a lovely mum. You've got Jude. You've even – nng – got me, like it or not. And you've got your grandfather.'

Hal turned away. 'Him! I don't count him as family.'

'But he is. Close family. He may have been a miserable old sod, but he knows that now. Regrets it. I know – Hal, believe me, I know – what that feels like. Go on, give the old boy another chance.'

'He wasn't racist, like I thought,' Hal conceded. 'He didn't know.'

Don was putting his brushes to soak in a jam-jar, wiping his hands on a piece of filthy rag. 'No, he was just a stubborn, short-sighted old git.'

'Obstinate, Aunt Jude says.'

'Well, there you are then. He's got a lot to make up for, hasn't he? He wants to, really wants to. I think I'm done for today.' He reached down to the stack of boards and canvases. 'Here. This is for you.' He handed Hal a package wrapped in a carrier bag. 'Don't unwrap it now. Later.'

'But what—?'

'Wait till you get home. D'you mind leaving me alone for a bit? I've got to write this wretched speech for tomorrow night.'

When Hal got home, Mum and Aunt Jude were cooking

in the kitchen. Aunt Jude was stirring a saucepan, while Mum had her hands in a mixing-bowl, making crumble.

Hal showed them the package. 'Look, Don's given me this.'

'Oh, what?' Mum tried to uncrumble her hands, and leaned over to see.

'Looks like a picture.' Hal tore at the parcel tape.

It was a small unframed painting. With a shock, Hal recognised himself, head and shoulders, against the night sky. The angle was an unusual one, as if looking at him close over his shoulder, seeing his hair, his ear, the side of his cheek, one eye open and gazing, the inside of the lashes. Torch-glow showed his skin brown and gleaming, his lips parted, a glimpse of teeth. And above him the stars blazed, larger than life, flaring against ink-darkness. The shapes of garden trees swirled vaguely in the background.

'It's the other night in the garden,' Hal said. They stood, all three of them, gazing at the painting he held in his hands.

'Oh, it's lovely, lovely,' said Aunt Jude. 'And he's signed it, look! That must mean he's pleased with it. He only signs the ones he really likes.'

Mum gazed and gazed. 'It's beautiful! We'll get it framed, Hal, and you must keep it for ever.'

Hal turned the board over, and read *Hal and the Stars. Don Inchbold*. It sent an odd kind of tingle down his back, seeing himself like that, so close, so real. As if he was back there in the garden, in the cold autumn air. And as if Don knew him better than he knew himself.

He wondered how to say thank you for something so special.

The opening of the Lifeboat Gallery had a Hallowe'en theme. Pumpkin masks grinned from every spare surface; orange flames licked at the windows; bats fluttered in the rafters. A jazz band played, and down on the beach, a bonfire waited to be lit. It was a fine, starlit night, drawing lots of people.

Wesley was there. When Hal saw him come in, his heart thumped with stupid expectation, even though there was nothing to expect. When Wesley saw Hal's mum, and she saw him, there was a moment of shocked recognition. They greeted each other with a clasp of hands that turned into a hug, with lots of laughing; each said how well the other was looking, and Wesley said that Tina had a son to be proud of, and introduced them both to Valerie and his little girls. Then he and Mum began talking as if they had only tonight to catch up with all the years since they'd last seen each other. Soon Aunt Jude interrupted, reminding Mum that she wasn't to stand for too long, and mustn't get tired.

Luke was there, with his dad. 'Sailing tomorrow? Meet you down at the marina?'

Czeszka was there, with Gregor and her father, to whom she introduced Hal. Gregor, very smart in a black bow tie, was a waiter, carrying trays of wine and things to nibble.

Amanda Farman was there, elegant in a black dress, with piled-up hair. Don was there, sloshing wine, shuffling his feet, looking as if he'd rather be somewhere else.

And *Moony* was there, in pride of place on the wall of

the new extension. It looked right. It commanded attention with its brilliance and boldness. Some of the guests recognised it; Hal heard Don's name mentioned, more than once. 'Is that *him*? Over there by the door?' Others stood and studied the painting in silence.

More and more people were coming in, filling the space. After a hubbub of greetings and chatter, there were speeches to be made from a microphone. A local councillor, an MP, someone from the Arts Council. Then Amanda Farman stepped forward and gave a nervous cough.

'We're tremendously thrilled and honoured to have such a distinguished guest this evening, an artist who lives and works locally but who is known and admired internationally. Don Inchbold made a name for himself as one of the most striking painters of the nineteen sixties . . .'

Don, standing nearby, stared at the floor. He looked rather as Hal had felt in the Year Head's office, called in to give an account of himself.

'. . . very, very kindly agreed to loan us his most famous painting, *Moony,* and how stunning it looks . . .'

Don glanced up and caught Hal's eye; gave the smallest grin; looked down again and rubbed one shoe against the other trouser leg.

'. . . and I can't tell you how delighted I am that he's agreed to say a few words this evening. Please, let's show our appreciation. Don Inchbold.'

Cameras flashed as Don shambled up to the mike and spent some while adjusting it. Everyone waited.

'The Lifeboat Gallery,' Don said at last. 'Good name. Good place. I like it. Kuh! Because art is a lifeboat. Course it is. For me. For lots of people.' He gazed at the ceiling. 'Nnng.'

Dropping his arms to his sides, he looked around for Aunt Jude, then abruptly walked back to his place. It took several moments for people to realise he'd finished, then applause broke out, and polite laughter. 'Well, she said it'd be a *few* words,' someone said, behind Hal.

Amanda Farman declared the gallery officially open, invited everyone to wander, and reminded them that the bonfire was about to be lit. Don looked dazed. Aunt Jude went straight to him and took his arm, protecting him from the journalists who gathered round. 'Just a few questions, Mr Inchbold, if you don't mind? Art is a lifeboat? Can you expand on that? And *Moony*? Where's it been hidden, all these years, and how did you get it back? Are you living in Ryton now? Are you planning to exhibit again?'

It was Aunt Jude who answered. 'No, no plans. Possibly. Maybe.'

'Mr Inchbold! Have you completed any new work since you've been in Ryton?'

Don raised his head.

'Yes. Yes, I have. *Hal and the Stars,* it's called.'

'*Hal and the Stars*?' The reporter wrote it down. 'Can you tell us a bit more? A small hint? Will we see it on display here?'

'Maybe. Maybe not.' Don met Hal's eye. 'It's up to Hal, what happens to it.'

Outside, on the shingle, the blaze was catching hold: flames leaping, sparks flying up into the sky. There were fireworks, and hot drinks. Don went home to his flat, exhausted by his public appearance. Mum sat on the life-boat ramp, Aunt Jude beside her; Hal went down to the tide's edge with Luke and Czeszka, and skimmed stones, trying to outdo each other. Gradually the two boys deferred to Czeszka, copying her technique. It wasn't a matter of strength. Czeszka chose her stones carefully, selecting flat-sided ones, rubbing her thumb over the smooth flint. She angled herself at the incoming tide, narrowed her eyes, waited for the right moment. Then she gave a swift flick of her wrist, skilful as a spin-bowler, and the stone scudded along a flattening wave-top in more bounces than anyone could count. Hal saw Luke changing his opinion of Czeszka. He'd thought she was just a girl, a hanger-on. Now he wanted to impress *her*.

Later, when Luke and Graham left, Hal went in search of Mum. She was still there on the ramp, huddled into her coat, Aunt Jude beside her. Both looked extremely pleased with themselves.

'Hal, how would you feel about coming here to live?' Mum asked him.

'Here? Where? How?'

'Here in Ryton.'

'What, you mean like really *live* here? You and me?'

Hal thought of what this would mean. Not leave the sea after all? Be here all the time? Go down to the beach whenever he felt like it? Know the tides like he knew the days of the week? Learn to sail properly?

'You'd have to change school. Make new friends,' said Mum. 'But you'd still have Luke – he's down here quite often. And Czeszka now. And Osman could come and stay.'

'Stay *where*? What, we'd live with, uh, the grandfather?'

'No.' Mum gave a sidelong glance at Aunt Jude.

'We've been plotting.' Aunt Jude stretched out her hands to the bonfire's warmth. 'I want to help out. And I want you to help *me* out, which you would be doing.'

'Huh?' Hal looked from one to the other.

'I had a share in Marborough's,' said Aunt Jude, 'and I'd been thinking what to do with the money. A seaside place like this, it gets taken over with holiday cottages, and the prices go sky high. So it's hard for the locals to find places to live, let alone afford to buy. I've been looking at a pair of old cottages – I'm going to buy them and do them up, and rent them out to local people. I've already put in an offer.'

'Yeah,' Hal said, not quite following.

'So your mum can work for *me,* for a bit, now she's got no job at JJ's. Painting, decorating and so on. Till she finds something better. And then – well, *you're* local people, aren't you? At least your mum is. Born and brought up here. So you can be my first tenants.'

'It's really kind of you to help,' Mum said, but Aunt Jude waved away her thanks.

'Nonsense! It's for my own selfish pleasure. I'll enjoy having the cottages, and even more I'll enjoy having you two living close by. We'll be a proper family at last. I can't tell you how good that'll be.'

'You don't need to,' Mum said, smiling. 'And I can always be a mobile hairdresser. I'll earn my keep, mine and Hal's. I want to stand on my own two feet.'

'Course you do,' Aunt Jude agreed. 'Course you will.'

Mobile hairdresser? Hal imagined a van parked by the roadside, Mum cutting and styling in a lay-by, but she saw his puzzled look and said, 'Doing people's hair in their own homes. Lots of people prefer that, or can't get out for one reason or another. I'd advertise locally and I bet I'd soon find as much work as I wanted.'

Aunt Jude gave a contented sigh. 'And I'll stay where I am, if Gerry's happy with that. There's no point him rattling round that big house by himself. He needs me to keep him in order. Then Don can have the flat. We'll go on much the same as we are.'

'But what d'you think, Hal?' Mum was looking at him keenly. 'Do you like the idea?'

'Yes,' he said, and found that he meant it. 'Yeah! It's well cool.'

'Good,' Mum said, laughing.

'So – that's it, then?' Hal tried to take it in. 'We're not going home?'

'Oh, we'll go back for a few weeks at least,' said Mum. 'JJ's isn't closing till the end of November, and I'll need the money. There'll be loads to sort out. And we'll need to get you into a good school.'

Typical adult! You'd think school was the only thing that mattered. Hal thought of the homework he still hadn't quite finished, and the Anger Management that awaited him. *Anger Management!* What was that all about? He'd had it with anger. Anger had burned through him, and fizzled itself out. He couldn't remember, now, how it had felt.

'So,' he said hopefully, 'there's not much point going in on Monday, is there? If I'll be leaving so soon?'

He knew from the cynical smile on Aunt Jude's face and the wry look on Mum's that he had no chance of getting away with that. None at all.

22
GONE

Hal woke up, late, and instantly remembered that this was his last day. Tomorrow and school already loomed, but he pushed them out of his thoughts. Today mattered more.

And it wasn't really the end; he and Mum would soon be back. Down for weekends, sorting things out, helping Aunt Jude. Meeting the grandfather. There'd be lots to do.

'Like having a sort-out at home,' Mum told him. 'Goodness knows what's in your bedroom cupboard, Hal. Or mine, come to that. We'll take a load of stuff to the charity shop. Then when we move, we won't be wading through clutter.'

A new start, Hal thought. A new school, where he didn't have a reputation, where he hadn't been in trouble, and wouldn't go looking for it. Maybe he'd even have a friend there – Mum, on Aunt Jude's advice, had said she'd try for Southdean, where Czeszka was starting next week. She'd be in the same year, so there'd be at least one person he knew. As long as no one started on about her being his *girl*friend.

He'd arranged to meet Czeszka down on the beach.

'Your last day,' she'd said. 'We make something one last time.'

'For now,' he corrected.

The phrase puzzled her. 'Yes, for now, if you say.'

From habit, before setting off, Hal reached for the bag of marbles to select one. Then he had a better idea, and stowed the whole bag in his rucksack. Mum had made him a packed lunch, so that he could go straight on to the marina to meet Luke.

Czeszka was waiting for him, down by the beach huts. It was sunny but cold today, a chill wind cutting across from the east.

The early morning's high tide hadn't left many gifts. They began collecting what they could: a piece of plank, a Coke can, a flip-flop sandal. Nothing to inspire, nothing to spark an idea. And Hal felt that today they should make something special: a finale, a farewell, until he came back. A heap of old tat, as Don might put it, just wouldn't do.

They went farther along the beach and looked at the way the sun threw their shadows long and thin on the sand.

'Stand, please!' Czeszka told him. She'd picked up a flint. Bending, she traced the outline of Hal's shadow with its sharp edge until he was there, scored into the sand, a long slim boy. He quite liked the look of himself.

'Now you! My turn.' He picked up a sharp-edged stone and bent to draw round Czeszka's shadow. But she teased him, striking poses, dancing away, refusing to be captured and pinned down. Hal gave up, throwing away the piece of flint.

Instead, he began scooping damp sand with both hands: heaping and smoothing, patting. Moulding, sculpting and firming. At first, Czeszka stood and watched; then, as she saw that it was a sandman, she dug and piled too, taking the role of helper, letting Hal guide the way the figure was growing.

The sandman they made was life-size and sturdy. Big arms reached down his sides. Flat feet splayed out. His eyeless face looked up at the sky.

Czeszka looked expectantly at Hal. 'Eyes? You have?'

Hal remembered that all the marbles were in his ruck-sack. He pulled out the bag, reached in at random and gave the sandman one orange eye and one green. Then he placed a whole row of marble-buttons down the man's front. He gave him marble cufflinks, two on each sleeve. He shaped a hat, and put five marbles on top for a bobble. The two moons, his favourites, became ear-studs. Czeszka laughed, and Hal gave her the remaining marble, a ruby-red one. She held it, considering, then placed it on the man's clumpy hand, where it became the gem of a ring.

They both stood looking at the man they'd made. His life would be short; the incoming waves were already lapping his feet. He lay there like a sacrificial victim. Hal and Czeszka waited, silent and expectant. Foam bubbles melted into the sand. Then the sea sighed and pushed forward again, leaving a new fringe of surf.

'But the marbles!' Czeszka reached for the ruby-red ring, but Hal caught her arm, stopping her.

'No. Leave it. Leave all of them. I don't want them.'

Her eyes searched his face. She made another move, as if

to pluck a marble for herself; then, with a little shrug, she left it. She stood watching with Hal. A wave lifted and curled and fell, pushing farther up the sandman's body.

Hal let the waves hypnotise him, fill his mind.

Like this it would be, for ever and for ever. Thousands, millions, even billions of years into the future, until the Earth got swallowed up by the sun or went spinning into space. The moon making the tides rise and fall. Rock being pounded into sand. People – for as long as there *were* people – looking out to sea. Wishing. And wondering.

'The sea can make you mad,' Don had said. 'And the sea can make you sane.' Hal hadn't known what this meant, but now perhaps he did.

If you stood in one place, you could see how the tide was coming in. You could stand as close as possible to the water's edge and feel your shoes sinking into sand and grit as each wave washed back. Moments later you'd have to leap back or have your trainers filled with water and your jeans soaked.

Hal did this a few times, and so did Czeszka, until their jeans were tide-marked and their trainers drenched. Each time, they ran back laughing, stumbling, deliberately leaving it a little too late.

Hal had forgotten to watch the sandman being licked and dissolved. Now, he saw that the first marbles were being taken by the sea – lifted, rolled, sucked into the undertow. They became pebbles on the beach, then were lost in the next wave. Hal watched them go. Maybe he'd save the moon-marbles, keep just those two, put them safely in his pocket; but as he reached out his hand, his mind changed itself, and he left them.

For a few moments, the sandman's head was the only

part of him to be seen above the shine of water on sand; his nose pointing upward, his marble eyes in which Hal fancied – for just a second – there might be a sorry look. Then the wave washed right over his features, and the last two marbles rolled down into the foam.

The sea could take them. And the sea could take the sandman. Hal watched until there was nothing left to see.

'Gone,' said Czeszka.

'Yes. All gone.'

Hal thought that he could make another sandman, one day, any day, whenever he chose. But he never would. And he didn't even feel regretful, not now.

'Come on,' he said to Czeszka, turning his back. 'It's too cold to hang around.'

Time to go sailing.

ACKNOWLEDGEMENTS

With thanks to all the people who have helped in various ways: in particular Margaret Taylor and Chris at Henry Cort Community School; to Tony and Heather Birr of Firstaway Yacht Charters, for a memorable weekend on the Solent; to Black Boys Can (www.blackboyscan.co.uk) for various insights, and to the group from Sherfield School at The Hurst Arvon Centre in March 2008, for a refresher course in Year Nineness. Also to Trevor, for support; and to Ian Benfold Haywood, whose illustrations add so much to the book. And, as ever, to Jon Appleton, for excellent editing and guidance.

ABOUT THE AUTHOR

Linda Newbery is the Nestlé Silver Award-winning author of *Catcall*, and of *Set in Stone,* winner of the 2006 Costa Children's Book Award – in addition to more than thirty other books for readers of all ages.

Linda wanted to be an author from the age of eight. She now writes full-time from her home in Northamptonshire, and is much in demand as a speaker in schools and libraries and at festivals and conferences.